Also by Lance C Wilson

THE LAIRD OF BRAIDWOOD
Historical

TEARS OVER THE KIMBERLEYS

DARE TO LIVE THE DREAM

THE CHILDREN OF KIMBERLEY COTTAGE
BILLY OF THE NORTH
MY FIELD OF DREAMS

THE STONE PEOPLE

DARK SIDE OF THE ROCK

THE GULF

MEG'S STORY
FIFTY ACHES AND PAINS

PAULINE'S JOURNEY
LANCE C WILSON

Come on a journey with Pauline - an inspiring journey of discovery, sexual awakening and womanhood.

Printed and published by Kimberley Cottage Publishing

This is a work of Adult Fiction.

All characters and events are portrayed fictitiously.

National Library of Australia Cataloguing-in-Publication entry:

Author: Wilson, Lance C, 1945

Title: Pauline's Journey

Editor: Rhonda Scott JP

Cover photo by Stephan Miechel

Cover design and book layout by Alan Jennison

ISBN: 9780 – 977 – 550 – 586

Dewey No. A 823.4

A CiP record for this book is available from the National Library of Australia

Many Thanks

To my friend Rhonda Scott for her tireless efforts in editing
the raw manuscript of my novel and bringing it to life

To Stephan Miechel for the magic of his photography

To Alan Jennison for turning Stephen's photo into an
eye- catching cover and for making the edited novel print ready

and

Special Thanks

To my wife Cynthia for always being there!

Foreword

Pauline Joy Brown was born in Canberra, the public service capital of Australia, to career public servants Bruce and Jane Brown. Bruce who happened to believe anyone outside Canberra were imbeciles unable to function without intervention from thousands of rules and regulations ably administered from the capital by them, assisted by mega departments spewing out so many rules and regulations no one knew exactly from where they came or how to stop them.

Pauline started and finished her education in Canberra. On completion she was assured a position in the public service simply because of the old boys' network existing amongst the elite with whom her parents socialised. Because of rules and regulations the position was advertised but truth be told Pauline was already drawing a salary.

Raised in the absolute unreality of public service speak and thousands of meetings, reports and white papers - or any other paper - she soon became opinionated and an expert in buck-passing and bullshitting

Living at home, the only world she really knew was attending meetings to justify her position somehow and blending into the bloated system.

At the age of thirty five she was still a virgin and because of her sedate and boring lifestyle she was overweight.

One of her biggest moments of fame was when, standing behind a politician crapping on, she began bobbing her head up and down like a maniac whilst the Honourable Member delivered a stirring speech which Pauline was aware was total bullshit. However she believed without her and her thousands of associates, society would collapse without the expert guidance they slaved away delivering.

Her actual experience with the opposite sex was a slap on the arse from a co-worker years before followed by weeks of counselling and the perpetrator having to complete six months of lectures in work place etiquette. No hope existed for Pauline or co-workers ever getting into a relationship in such a sterile environment - to even look at the opposite sex was taboo.

However when Pauline met a new female employee the event changed her life and a trip around Australia introduced her to the real world, a sexual awakening, and finally love and lust in the dust.

Pauline's true character would surface - a fantastic journey.

Chapter One

A cold wind cut through the bleak suburb of Chifley as Pauline, busting for a pee, lay prone in bed waiting for her father to finish his morning ablutions. A career public servant, now a department head who thought up stupid ways to spend taxpayer money was so dreadfully, and painfully slow, preparing for work that Pauline dreaded the morning ritual.

Pauline knew her mother would have two pieces of toast and coffee ready, for it was Tuesday - toast day. Her father was a stickler for organisation and anything outside the regimented life he led sent him into major panic. Once she remembered his car breaking down on the way to work, the incident sent him into a blind panic and he dialled '000' giving rise to the ire of the operator, when informed of the problem. The result was three weeks of trauma counselling and his instructing a Solicitor to proceed against the car dealer, which of course was immediately stopped on learning her father had run out of petrol.

The department he ran had grown from thirty to now hundreds, even he was unsure how many. Being so full of his own importance he simply arranged meetings delegating responsibility to department heads while he spent most of the time organising a women's basketball team and applying for sporting grants. Pauline was to learn later in life he was actually a pervert and this facilitated his fetish

9

along with watching porn in his office whenever possible.

Pauline's gaunt looking mother, always nervous because of her marriage environment, worked in the Prime Minister's office arranging hotel rooms and other travel arrangements. A trusted employee, she covered many an indiscretion on many of the junkets she organised for senior politicians on fact finding missions. One wag, slightly pissed at a function described them as 'fuck finding missions'.

Although Jane, since marriage had never been on a holiday or left Canberra, her husband went on many government meetings in various states but she knew he was busy screwing prostitutes on these trips. She dreaded every Saturday before he went off to manage his basketball team. This was 'suck cock morning', no doubt to stop him becoming too excited when managing the team. The advent of Viagra made him harder to bring off and a lot stiffer to get it over with, so she often had to mount him and vigorously fuck him, always in dread of what his dick had been up on his last trip. She had medical checks monthly, to the amusement of her GP who wondered why a woman married to a respected Public servant need bother!

Pauline sighed, at last the loo was vacant and rushing in she plonked herself onto the seat as a great gush of pee hit the water below making a noise like a monster wave crashing onto rocks. Now thirty five and bored shitless with her life even she began to see the whole Canberra scene was lifeless, a town of false people all full of their own importance. She longed for some excitement or satisfaction other than stuffing herself each day with food she knew was unhealthy and adding to her body weight. Pauline felt she was in a tunnel, unsure and with no direction especially from her parents who both seemed so boringly predictable that each hour was planned without variation in the day to day life they tragically adhered to.

Pauline had threatened to leave home once but her mother sobbed and collapsed at the thought, so she relented. She also knew rents were high in Canberra and at home she was saving all her money and had a large nest egg. Mum supplied all the food and was always buying her clothes, although now, tent-like dresses.

Pauline had no car but she had learnt to drive and was licensed. Her father lectured her on the inconvenience of two vehicles in the driveway, so important was his job that he may have to go into work at any time. This had never occurred in the fifteen years Pauline had been working but as always forward planning was paramount in her father's life.

Her parents having already left for work, she locked the door and waddled the short distance to the bus stop. She plopped onto the bus seat nearly knocking a girl over, whose eyes were glued to the phone she was holding as she perched on the edge of the seat. Arriving at work she realised in dismay she had forgotten her security tag - a major incident in this part of the country, even though the security officers knew her and had checked her tag for ten years. The behaviour of all was on par with Osama Bin Laden arriving. An irritated department head had to attend and vouch for Pauline along with dozens of official looking documents having to be filled in and countersigned. In fact two hours later she was finally admitted, vowing if she ever found herself again in this predicament she would go home and take a sickie - far less stressful for dozens of people as well as saving thousands in lost time and paperwork.

Immediately she went to the cafeteria and ordered a strong coffee and two doughnuts lashed with cream thinking it may ease her headache. She was seated on her own as usual and a tall skinny girl whom she knew was a newcomer sat and joined her, a surprise to Pauline - no one joined boring old Pauline.

"How ya goin, my name is Sophie. Only arrived in this shit-hole yesterday - what a boring bunch of fuckers this lot is" Sophie informed her, sucking on a large milkshake as though she had been in the desert for weeks and was dying of hunger and thirst.

Pauline, wide eyed and absolutely overwhelmed by the intrusion and behaviour of her visitor lied in reply, "Pauline pleased to meet you".

"Met a new boyfriend last night, Abdul - have a job to sit down, we screwed all night" Sophie blurted out between loud slurps. Pauline felt like slipping under the table as others nearby glanced at the pair inquisitively.

Trying to be dignified Pauline replied "Actually, have a bad headache myself. I had a problem this morning, forgot my security tag."

"Fuck me what the hell would be a major problem with that? Oh shit of course, this is fucken Canberra" Sophie replied.

"Protocol must be adhered to Sophie" Pauline replied.

"Oh well Pauline old girl better get back to the bullshit, got some wanker giving me an induction course. Seems it's gonna take a month to learn me how to take paper from one fucking desk to another! See ya" Sophie replied as she plonked the milkshake down and skipped off leaving a shocked Pauline watching her departure wondering how she had indeed landed a job in the same building as her in Canberra.

Pauline arrived at her desk wondering how she would fill the day in with no major cost cutting projects on her desk to deal with but smiled and was glad as she felt quite ill.

Pauline's last big job resulted in 'savings' she had arranged by sacking four tea ladies. No job losses in her department were even considered.

She in fact transferred the four tea ladies to the new cafeteria she designed and had built at a cost of four million on the third floor plus the appointment of consultants and advisors on the project at a further cost of six hundred thousand. The cafeteria was convenient to all but now no tea lady visited each floor and another two staff were needed to run it, effectively resulting in the cost of an extra six wages. This, in addition to the millions spent building and outfitting it and the additional power costs and other outgoings incurred in running a large cafeteria.

Still all her superiors seemed happy at the results as did the four tea ladies who did not have to push a cart from floor to floor, room to room. All the workers too congratulated Pauline. A wider range of food was now available, not the boring tea and biscuits.

Pauline viewed the project as a triumph and successful

13

cost cutting measure having transferred all costs to another department and saving four wages, a brilliant shuffle satisfactory to all.

It had taken Pauline two years and kept her focused. Now she waited for her next departmental cost cutting job, as did her seven staff.

So distressing had her failure to bring the security tag and the meeting with Sophie been, Pauline, now sitting at her desk trying to look busy along with her seven staff, decided to go home, take a Panadol and rest. Picking her bag up she informed her second in command of her decision and left the building to catch a bus. She arrived home and after taking two tablets crashed onto the bed heaving a huge sigh of relief.

Pauline was nearly dozing off when she heard a car drive in the drive and, peering through the window, saw it was her father's. 'Strange' she thought, 'it was unlike her father to come home during the day' and then she noticed Rita, the coach of the basketball team he managed, was with him, a big-titted, bottle-blonde, whose husband also worked in her department. Pauline lay back on the bed thinking they may have called in for papers or something to do with the basketball team. The reality of the situation changed when, after some time of cups clinking in the kitchen and the pair talking loudly, Pauline realised they were both banging about in her parents' bedroom across the hall, "Fuck me harder" Rita screamed. Pauline sat upright on her bed in complete shock.

Sneaking to her door she opened it slowly just enough to see the bedroom. The door had been left wide open and clothes, pants and bra lay on the floor, even in the passage. Rita was laying naked on the bed, her arms flapping about like a wounded duck. In complete oblivion to the fact they were being watched, her father, leaning over the side of the bed with Rita's legs wrapped around him, was pumping frantically into a screaming Rita.

Closing the door, Pauline staggered back to the bed collapsing, unsure what to do. She tried to cover her ears but the groaning and banging across the hall was hard to block out. Pauline felt sick.

She had always perceived her father as being perfect and had even looked down sometimes on her mother for constantly ostracising him. She somehow seemed weak and indecisive. Her father was her rock. Even though no close relationship had ever formed, from a distance she admired him. Always in total control, his advice she always considered correct in all details. Now he was across the hall fucking big-titted Rita like a wild animal while she screamed obscenities and for him to fuck harder.

Pauline now had a bigger headache. In fact she was devastated. Cocooned in her own little world, the reality had hit her like a cyclone. Quietly she lay for at least two hours until she heard them dressing and leave closing the door behind them. Pauline still lay pondering what she had just observed then she decided to say nothing. Her mother would be shattered and the marriage, and indeed her family, would disintegrate. 'No' Pauline thought, 'say nothing'.

Again she was dozing when her father pulled up in his car. She listened as he made a phone call telling her mother he was home feeling sick and to come home on the bus. She heard the shower go and her father close the bedroom door then all went quiet.

Later her mother returned home and she heard her father get up and go to the kitchen. "The Viagra is on the table" she said to him, "it's not Saturday morning!" He replied, "Stupid woman, it's also good for headaches, everyone knows that" as Pauline heard the door slam.

Pauline then for the first time in her life decided perhaps all her father told her, and indeed her mother, may not absolutely be correct.

Pauline sneaked to the front door opening it. She closed it loudly and went to her room closing it too so both parents heard, knowing they would consider her just arriving home from work.

The incident had indeed changed Pauline's mindset, now her father was not infallible and this caused her to think about the meeting with Sophie that morning, maybe she should foster the relationship! Sophie delivering documents to all her departments and indeed others would be a good source of information. 'Yes' Pauline mused, 'life can change, perhaps my blinkered view on life is not as correct as it seems'. Pauline felt invigorated. In fact a new era of her life was about to commence.

Chapter Two

The following morning security tag in hand, Pauline arrived at work purposely waiting around the cafeteria for Sophie to arrive. A frown came over her forehead, had she been sacked already? Then she reckoned that no one gets sacked from the public service, just counselled and retrained.

Five minutes later on cue Sophie swept into the cafeteria. Pauline followed her in greeting her with a big smile, pointing to a vacant table. They both sat down, assured no one else would join them.

"How are things going Sophie? Hope you are settling in" Pauline chirped.

"As well as can be expected, fuck I thought I was made getting this job. A politician owed Dad a favour and got it for me" Sophie grinned back.

"What does your dad do?" Pauline asked.

"Dad was a copper, must've known something about the sleazy prick who got me this gig" was the reply.

"This your first job, Sophie?" Pauline asked, knowing not to go too far too fast.

"Nah" Sophie replied, "worked my way round Australia, mostly in roadhouses and picking fruit. Had a ball. That was the real world, this is fucken fantasyland".

"Why did you come home?" Pauline asked.

"Well Dad met this fucken moll after Mum died and she was a real schemer. Talked him into selling his

17

house and giving her all his money to start up a business supposedly to make them a fortune! Well she got the cash and fucked off. Dad an ex-copper too! He is now in an aged care facility and I am renting. Dad is fucked, it finished him, so I will stay and visit him until he dies, owe the old bugger that" Sophie replied.

Pauline began to see that under Sophie's rough exterior a good person existed, not false and self-centred like many she worked with. She intrigued her more each time they met.

Pauline and Sophie became good friends and even met after work for a meal several times. One evening Sophie turned up with Abdul and introduced him to Pauline.

"Pauline this is Abdul, he has just asked me to marry him" Sophie beamed. Abdul was very polite and shook Pauline by the hand like a true gentleman.

"We are getting married in a registry office Pauline. Will you attend me and be my witness? Sophie enquired. Although Pauline had reservations she did accept and was informed the wedding was the following weekend.

The next day as they sat down to morning tea, now a ritual, Pauline asked, "What does Abdul do for a living?"

Sophie replied, "The poor boy is on a scholarship to university, he is sponsored by an aid organisation. His family are goat herders, he wants to stay here and eventually sponsor them out. Oh Pauline, his poor mother Fatwa has thirteen children and Abdul wants so badly to help them."

"Are you sure this is a good idea Sophie, have you thought this through?" Pauline asked her.

"Of all people Pauline, I didn't think you'd be a racist,

please don't spoil my happiness" Sophie shot back.

"Sophie I am no racist, just being a good friend, believe me" Pauline replied.

"I knew you would understand Pauline, you are a true friend" Sophie responded.

Pauline never mentioned the matter again but let Sophie bask in her happiness. Sophie told her Abdul had moved in with her and she was paying the rent and assisting him with spending money as he was working hard at university. In fact she said he was taking courses after uni to help with his studies and that she was so proud of him. She added that she understood they would have no social life until his courses had been completed but was happy to help and at home he was attentive and a wonderful lover, nothing was taboo in his sexual practices, it was all so exciting.

The following weekend Pauline as promised attended the civil ceremony and was surprised that Abdul arrived alone with no fellow countrymen to witness such a special event in his life. Sophie, Pauline and one of Sophie's workmates seemed the only people who would be present to witness the happy occasion. Pauline thought it strange that immediately after the event, Marriage Certificate in hand 'poor Abdul had to leave to attend a weekend course'!

Pauline and Sophie sat alone sipping a coffee marking the momentous day. Sophie, so proud of her hard working Abdul, so dedicated to their future was he that he devoted all his life at this time to his studies. Pauline had to pay for the coffee and cake because Sophie had to give Abdul, her husband of five minutes, all her spare cash in order for him to buy food and other essentials needed for the additional weekend course he was attending.

Pauline left Sophie at the business she worked evenings and weekends at to supplement her public service salary. As the sole bread winner she was happily working at two jobs to allow Abdul to pursue his studies. By doing so she informed Pauline he would finish sooner and then take over the responsibility of being the family provider.

Pauline also noticed from that time Sophie did not seem to mention the magnificent sex life she and Abdul had enjoyed. Arriving home late after studies it appeared he was now too tired to participate in the frantic lovemaking they enjoyed prior to their marriage.

Pauline did not have a great deal of time to dwell on the matter as on the Monday the new Labor Prime Minister, because of the world financial situation, decided to start a spending stimulus in order to save Australia from impending disaster as other governments worldwide, who had spent like drunken sailors, faced the reality that debt had to be serviced and at some time repaid. The banking system also, with shonky borrowers heading to the hills, turned to taxpayers to bail them out.

A senior bureaucrat, at a meeting with the PM, who swore lots, was arrogant and considered himself 'God's gift to the nation' in a bold effort to avoid the workload he knew was coming to splash billions of taxpayer dollars about, remembered the wonderful job Pauline Joy Brown had done in wasting millions saving her department money in the 'Tea Lady' incident. In fact it was his only recollection of anyone doing or achieving anything in his time as a bureaucrat, so he lavished praise on Pauline to escape any responsibility himself and be seen as having made a decision.

And so Pauline found herself sitting meekly in the office of the PM whilst he outlined his great vision for saving the nation. 'Fuck the cost, just do it' and he would give her all the staff and assistance needed, failure was not an alternative. That afternoon Pauline had her staff increased by one hundred and she was elevated to the position of a department head. She even requested Sophie be her assistant, knowing the pay rise would help her keep 'poor Abdul' in funds without, she hoped having to work seven days a week.

Several other department heads now sat before Pauline who told them of the massive spending programs that would in fact get underway immediately. 'Pink Batts' was one that would stimulate the economy and a hastily ill-conceived program began. Hundreds of unskilled and shonky installers, many of whom found it hard to believe their luck, simply threw Pink Batts into ceilings, even over electrical wires and other Pink Batts. Although rumblings of shonky practices, and fires caused through those practices, started to surface Pauline was in the clear, her department was only the instigator and all responsibility was simply passed on. Years in the system had taught her well.

The building program also made headlines. Building work worth a mere fifty thousand costing millions and some contractors simply pocketing the millions then passing the work on to the minor players. Pauline knew all this and leaving Sophie speechless, ploughed on. The

21

mission she was given was to 'save Australia', to spend all the savings of the previous government - in addition to the borrowed billions.

As the summer of discontent rose Pauline attended many meetings blaming every department head for the fiasco claiming they had mismanaged the money handed out to them and informing a fuming, swearing PM that it was simply the fault of those outside her jurisdiction who had fucked the whole thing up, truly Pauline's finest hour. Even Pauline's father told her how proud he was of her, a rare event. In the past he had considered her an embarrassment.

Pauline even allowed Sophie, trying to make herself more attractive to Abdul by experimenting with new hairstyles and brand clothing, entice her into attending hair salons and fashion shows.

Two events happened in the space of three weeks that shattered Pauline's world. Seated in her office on a Saturday morning as was now her practice during the revelations of spending taxpayer dollars as fast as possible, she was visited by two Police. A shocked Pauline learnt her father had been killed in a car accident as had the basketball coach Rita. Pauline wondered why one of the Police was unable to keep a straight face but after they left Sophie informed a distraught Pauline that Rita had got a bit carried away giving her father a head job and bit his cock causing the accident but luckily no one else was involved. Then the following week Sophie informed Pauline that tens of thousands of illegal images of teen and child porn were found on a private computer her father had in his office.

Still coming to terms with this flood of information Pauline was devastated but surprisingly her mother seemed to change overnight. After the funeral she had a cleanup throwing all her late father's belongings into a skip bin and waving goodbye to it as the crew she had hired disappeared down the road.

Pauline and her mother attended the reading of the Will. Pauline to her surprise was left the house and her mother, her father's money and super funds worth a considerable amount. Shocked, Pauline informed her mother she would sign the house over to her as she did not really want it.

Jane stared at Pauline, "Fuck the house Pauline, it's yours! I spent the most miserable fucking years under that roof, let me stay for long enough to make alternative arrangements and my greatest day will be walking out the front door never to look back. Your late father, if you have not heard, was a bloody pervert and dead shit. I wish I'd had the guts to leave the bastard years ago."

Jane also joined the girls on trips to the beauty salons and Pauline noticed a complete change in her mother. She even informed Pauline she was now transferring to the Minister of Agriculture's staff and would be accompanying him on interstate trips in the future. Sophie told Pauline that 'past favours had been called in'!

Chapter Three

Pauline now seemed to enjoy a much closer relationship with her mother who seemed to like Sophie also. Jane now spent time interstate as part of the official party and her confidence and personality changed much to Pauline's amazement.

Pauline attended constant meetings as the programs she was supplying funds to, seemed to be out of control. Seated next to Sophie as they awaited the PM at one such meeting she looked at Sophie, "What a bloody mess, a complete cock-up."

Sophie replied, "These fuckers are unable to do anything, they are all a bunch of morons. Take a look at all the billions wasted. They cannot deliver even the most basic services, useless pricks. Look Pauline, just watch your own fucking back."

"Bloody hell Sophie, I am beginning to believe you, it's all spin and bullshit" Pauline replied.

The waiting ended when a staff member informed them the PM would not be coming, the meeting had been cancelled. Pauline was glad, his swearing and blaming everyone for being incompetent, which they of course were, irritated her. This after all was the public service, used to quiet coffees and meetings and responsible for bugger all.

Later that day Pauline learnt the PM had been removed by a coup de grace by his Union backed Deputy, now she knew the spin and bullshit would reach a crescendo. The politicians, as Sophie informed her, are so far removed from the reality of the lives of ordinary Australians, life was about to become worse. Sophie, always one to give an opinion, informed Pauline that no one in Parliament had even run a fish and chip shop, yet they gave press conferences raving on about fiscal policy and all other catchy jargon, blissfully ignorant about what they crapped on about. Pauline soon found out things had changed. Her new job was cancelled because of her association with the previous PM and she once again returned to her job doing nothing out of favour. She knew this happened when political parties changed but usually not when it was just the leader.

Luckily Sophie was returned to her old position so Pauline had the satisfaction of having day to day news of what was really going on.

The following week Jane returned from a meeting with the Cattlemen's Association in the Kimberleys. Pauline wondered why her mother was so cheerful amongst the chaos in politics and stunned when Pauline tried to get her feelings on the knifing that had happened in the halls of democracy.

"Fuck them all, what democracy? Two self-serving, major political parties rule this country Pauline. Do you really think the members of either party represent their electorates or the stupid people who vote them in? For fuck's sake get real, democracy my arse!"

"Mum you sound like Sophie, but I am beginning to believe you" a stunned Pauline replied.

"By the way have you seen Sophie, I thought she might like to come to the salon with me this afternoon?" Jane asked.

"Sophie is working Mum. Abdul needs the money for his studies." Pauline responded.

"For fuck's sake, I thought Sophie was clever, the dumb bitch. That shithead married her so he can get Australian citizenship and then get his family out here on the fucking dole. Is she so bloody dumb? Study, my arse, he is mostly with his own people all the time enjoying life while she works her butt off" a fuming Jane informed a shocked Pauline.

"Mum now it adds up, for shit's sake, nothing is as it seems, this whole place is so false. We all live and work in an environment so false and corrupt it has taken me years to accept the reality of it all" Pauline replied.

"Pauline you are my daughter and I love you but I will be honest, I have met a station owner from the Kimberleys. He is on his own, we had a brief fling and he is coming down tonight to stay with us. I am going to give him the best time ever, bonk his brains out. Hopefully he will ask me back to his world and if so I will grab the opportunity with both hands" Jane replied laughing.

"Mum, are you serious?" Pauline asked, looking stunned.

"Never been so serious, my life has been shit and I need someone who wants me for what I am. We all need someone Pauline, about time you thought of that and got out of this fucking cesspool of backstabbing and greed" Jane replied.

At that time Sophie burst in "We have been kicked out

of the flat, poor Abdul had to send money home to his mother to feed the starving kids and did not pay the rent, he was too ashamed to tell me" Sophie sobbed.

"Reality check, Sophie my girl!" Jane replied grabbing her, "this piece of shit is stuffing your life for fuck's sake, the prick only wants citizenship through you and your fucking hard-earned money. Once he has that he will leave you."

"You are both jealous of me" wailed Sophie.

"Get real Sophie, I always thought you were clever, this prick has you sucked in" Pauline, now for once taking control, shouted at Sophie.

"He loves me Pauline" a sobbing Sophie blubbered.

"Okay Sophie, let's see how much Abdul loves you. Let's set up a scenario for him and let him prove it - or don't you want to know the truth?" Jane enquired sternly.

"How?" Sophie, now grasping the reality of her situation, asked.

"You will have to move here. I will get a removal truck and bring your gear here. Contact Abdul and tell him to come here and ask Pauline if it is okay for you to stay here for a few days. Make it for 2pm so we can set things up. Tell him you cannot leave work and have no money" Jane told her smiling, thinking of the audacity of the plan she had hatched.

"But I got sacked from work because I walked out when the agent told me they had locked the unit" Sophie sobbed.

"No problems, Abdul does not know that. We will be in the bedroom listening. Only Pauline, as far as he is concerned, will be here. Trust me girls, let's set the fucker up" Jane instructed them.

Sophie phoned Abdul who was furious she had phoned him on his mobile, even though she had purchased it for him and was paying the bill. Sophie informed him as instructed. She suggested Pauline may let them stay free of charge as she owned the house and was wealthy because of the millions, she repeated 'millions', left to her by her late father. Abdul's behaviour changed immediately, "Yes my precious wife, flower of the desert, I will attend to this unfortunate matter at once!"

"Now girls, both of you get some balls, wish I had years ago. I have an appointment at the salon so let's all go, we have to look better than sexy, especially you Pauline. Wear some revealing lingerie and when Abdul arrives be prancing around looking stunning but for fuck's sake get a Brazilian, you have more hair on your fanny than some women have on their head!" Jane informed the two stunned girls.

"What time is your new man coming Mum?" Pauline asked as they piled into her mother's car.

"His name is David Anderson and I have to pick him up at 5pm at the airport. Don't worry the Abdul affair will be over by then I promise, just do as I say." Jane was in her element. She had seen Abdul with friends on many occasions lazing about in the city when Sophie was working to give him extra money for studies. She knew he was a conniving piece of shit using a vulnerable young woman.

Jane visited the real estate agent paying Sophie's back rent and obtaining a key to collect her belongings the following morning. She knew Sophie would pay her back as promised. Jane also knew Sophie would be good company for Pauline if her own plans and wishes came to a satisfactory conclusion.

Two hours later the plot began to take shape. Pauline did have a nice face and although slightly chubby had huge breasts but now, wearing a see-through lace teddy, even Sophie was amazed at the transformation.

"Geez Pauline, you look hot! You know I thank both of you, I did not allow myself to face the reality of my situation. I had doubts that Abdul was doing as much study and after we married he cooled off with the attention and sex" Sophie gravely told her two confidantes.

Pauline was enjoying the moment. For the first time she felt really sexy. A beautiful hairstyle and makeup gave her a sense of empowerment and glancing in the mirror she gave her protruding breasts a lift and admired her shiny, smooth mound, barely visible behind the sheer material.

Jane had instructed Pauline to escort Abdul to the kitchen and they would be waiting in the pantry behind a heavy curtain. She also warned Sophie on threat of death that no matter what happened she was to wait until the time was right to make their dramatic entrance.

At the appointed time the bell rang and Jane and Sophie went to their positions. Pauline by now on such a high she was moist with anticipation and, revelling in the greatest moment of her life, swept the front door open, feigning absolute surprise, "Oh Abdul so sorry, I thought it was my mother, please forgive me - but now you have seen me please come in".

29

Abdul gulping for breath followed Pauline as she walked seductively to the kitchen. "Would you like a drink Abdul, what brings you here?" Pauline asked in her most seductive voice, watching Abdul stare at her breasts and his eyes stray below.

Abdul coughed and spluttered, "Pauline you see, Sophie has spent all our money and didn't pay the rent, silly woman. I make big mistake marrying her, should have marry someone like you."

"Oh, so what do you need me for Abdul?" Pauline, now in total control, crooned.

"So sorry, but can we move in here please for little while. I divorce stupid bitch when I get my citizenship and maybe marry you Pauline, very sexy lady" Abdul, swallowing hard and gulping, drooled.

"But you love Sophie" Pauline sweetly replied, thrusting her tits out.

"Never love stupid woman, love you Pauline. Perhaps me move in with you" Abdul, with his penis swelling, fighting to keep control, replied.

"What about all your studies Abdul? I would want a lover all the time, I need lots of fucking" Pauline, now going beyond her instructions, feeling absolutely in control and soaking wet, purred.

"Please Pauline, no study much at all. I have been with me friends but tell stupid woman me study. I fuck you big and perhaps you help me with money to send starving family" drivelled Abdul, now totally infatuated and already imagining counting the money.

"Well," Pauline sweetly replied "show me what you

have dearest Abdul and we can go to my bedroom, maybe."

Abdul tore off his clothes and standing naked, penis erect, unable to control himself lurched at Pauline, who in alarm turned around. Abdul grabbed her from behind and she felt his hardness push against the fabric of the lace teddy into her moist fanny. Looking up she saw her mother and Sophie sweep into the room as poor Abdul still erect and throbbing stood in absolute shock at a smiling Jane and screaming Sophie who grabbed a butcher's knife. Abdul swept up his clothes and tore out the front door and down the street with Sophie in hot pursuit.

Jane panicked and ran to the front gate but knew no one was going to catch poor Abdul who, in absolute terror with Sophie in pursuit, dropped all his clothing. Sophie stopped aware he was too fast but picking up his trousers and shirt neatly sliced them into strips before returning to the scene of the crime.

"Thanks girls, we need not mention this again, Sophie has learnt her lesson big time!" Sophie, now again in control, informed them both.

"Bloody hell Mum, I nearly got rogered by that prick. Did you have to leave it to the last minute?" Pauline, now beaming and aware of her sexuality for the first time, giggled.

"Well Sophie, and you Pauline, very few men would have turned that down but it was what he said that proved he was using you Sophie. What we have between our legs girls is a powerful weapon if used right. My life has taught me many lessons. If you just want a good ride fine, but choose a partner well. There are good men about but girls be warned, life is too short to waste it on liars and cheats." Jane pointed a finger at them both, laughing now but the ludicrous situation she had schemed suddenly hit her and she frowned at what may have happened.

"Mum I have decided to take Sophie out and to stay overnight so you can have a clear field to entertain David. I think we all need some space and time out" Pauline informed Jane and said "Sophie, never done this before in my life but let's drive over to Braidwood and spend the night in a B&B, it's on me." She had indeed decided on a new direction. Her acting out the drama had given her a new sense of power and raised her sexuality. She wanted to take it further.

Within the hour Pauline had packed, promising to buy Sophie some clothes at a shopping centre on the way. Sophie accepted. She needed to get away even for a short time, fully aware she would not see Abdul again. She would inform Immigration that the marriage was over and why.

Jane quickly cleaned up the house in preparation for David. He was a wonderful lover and she felt young again and in control, hoping it would lead to a new life far away from the back stabbing and falseness of Canberra. At 5pm she waited patiently and smiled as she watched him approaching, "Hi, did you have a good trip?" she asked.

"You look smashing, I have really thought of nothing else but you Jane since you left last week" David told her, clutching her hand.

"It's lovely to hear that David, actually the same here! I thought we might have an early meal on the way home.

Are you hungry?" Jane enquired.

"The only hunger I have is to get you naked in bed" David replied as he picked up his case from the conveyer belt.

A quiver went down Jane's back. She too was hungry for the intimacy they had shared. Turning, she gave him a peck on the cheek and upon reaching the vehicle they embraced with a passion, both knowing that only a serious session of sex would quell the fire raging between them.

Arriving at the house they entered and, like wild animals, tore the clothes off each other before falling onto the bed. Without any foreplay Jane wrapped her legs around him as he plunged into her, both thrusting in a frenzy, their lust knowing no bounds. Jane was dripping wet and reaching a mind blowing orgasm as they both collapsed, she felt the spunk shooting inside her. Still panting they looked at each other smiling. "I really needed that," David told her "to be honest I have thought of nothing else. Actually took a Viagra on the plane so we can go for it" he added.

"You men and your Viagra, what did you do before it came out?" Jane laughed.

"Well it lets us satisfy our partners and have multiple sex and really hard-ons" David laughed. He felt the swelling coming again as Jane fondled his penis, knowing she was going to have a night of real passion.

Several times during the long night they endured long sessions of pure lust, both hungry and eager to please each other. After one marathon Jane fathomed she had had more sex in that one evening than in any year of her marriage. She knew in David she had found a partner who would take her beyond the bounds of normality, nothing was taboo as both experimented on each other with sex sessions both had heard about but in the past had not dared try, now both hungry for new and exciting sexual adventures they both reached new heights of pleasure.

Jane was sound asleep when the phone rang. Rubbing her eyes she answered it, shocked that it was ten o'clock. It was Pauline. She and Sophie were at Sophie's old flat loading her belongings into the small truck ordered the day before. Jane was tickled to hear that Sophie had taken Abdul's belongings and tossed them in a skip at the tip.

Jane returned to the bedroom to find David waiting for her, penis again erect. "Good man," she exclaimed. "How many times can you get it up?"

"With you no boundaries Jane, you excite me, I cannot get enough of you" David replied, jumping out of bed, roughly laying her over the side and opening her legs, taking her in one wild push causing her to moan softly as his passion rose riding her like a wild bull, reaming in and out, his balls slapping against her buttocks, finally pulling out watching his sperm spurt over her belly, sweat dripping from his brow.

"Let's get cleaned up Tarzan." Jane smiled. The wilder and more erotic he treated her, the more she wanted, the fire of their aroused passion knowing no bounds.

He joined her in the shower, both slowly washing each other under the warm water. Jane gently washing his penis as he washed her vagina, lost in the moment, enjoying the sensual touching. Both sated for the time being, Jane knew she had found her man and mused about spending much more time with him as he skillfully ran his fingers gently into her swelling vagina.

The moment was broken when they heard a car pull up in the drive followed by another vehicle. Pulling on a dressing gown Jane walked to the door to find Pauline and Sophie getting out of the vehicle and a small truck parked behind.

Chapter Four

Pauline looked at her mother, "Mum you look like both a drowned rat and a cat coming out of the cream bowl." Pauline laughed.

"Truthfully, I have just been fucked so hard all night I have a job to pee" Jane said, beaming. Honestly girls get a decent man and get it on, don't waste your life like I did."

"Bloody hell Sophie, I cannot believe this is my Mum. Go Mum go!" Pauline added.

"How was Braidwood?" Jane asked.

Sophie replied, "Boring really, we checked out the museum and had a good meal but after yesterday it all seemed so dull."

"Hi, I'm David Anderson, need a hand?" Pauline looked as a grey-haired man came out and grabbed her mother who gave a squeal of delight. Pauline certainly saw what her mother liked about this man. Years in the harsh north gave him a weather-beaten look but he was all muscle, firm and, she guessed, fit also. He was interesting, unlike the men she was used to.

Jane informed them she was going to get dressed and show David around Canberra while the girls moved Sophie into the spare room.

"David informs me he is cooking the evening meal girls so we expect you both here by 6pm." Jane instructed.

Pauline, Sophie, David and the removal men stacked

Sophie's few belongings into the garage while Jane was heard singing happily in the bathroom, applying makeup and preparing for a day out with her new man. Pauline looked at the scene going on around her. Never in her entire life had she witnessed so much happening at her parents' home, even the lawn was mowed by a garden service in the past, everything was regimented. Actually, she began to comprehend just how regimented and boring life had been, no wonder her mother seemed so happy now.

Finishing, they waved the removals truck off. Even the two men had enjoyed the banter and laughed at Sophie's disposal of her husband's belongings. The job had been different and enjoyable. Seated around the kitchen table Pauline made coffee while David waited for her mother, preening and polishing herself up for her day of showing him around the capital.

Trying to make conversation Pauline cheerily asked, "How did you meet Mum, David?"

He replied sheepishly, "Well, I was having a meal with the Minister and about three hangers-on in Darwin. They were trying to be funny, telling the most politically correct, stupid jokes but no one was laughing. Actually it was boring so I told a joke and they all went white, glancing about as if someone might hear. I excused myself and went to the bar for a drink. None of the useless pricks would know a cow from a chook anyhow and there was your Mum, looking bored, also having a drink, so I joined her. We talked for hours and to be honest finished up in bed about midnight, so here I am. Your Mum is some woman Pauline, hope I can convince her to come home

37

with me, but I suppose she won't leave her job."

"Just ask her David, you might be surprised. By the way, what was the joke?" Pauline asked.

"I nearly forget it, an old Aboriginal tracker told me. He sounded so funny. I think it went like this:

A poetry competition was in progress and everyone had to think up a poem with the words "three" and "Timbuktu" in it. All these flash buggers got up and raved on with several poems, all so boring. Then old Jacky, who was at the back of the hall, staggered to the stage to recite his poem:

*"Me, and me mate Tim, down the road we went
and came across three gins in a tent.
So I 'buck' one and Tim 'buck' two."*

The politically correct bastards had been telling shit jokes about Poms and Scots all night - but mention Aboriginals or Muslims and they shit themselves."

Pauline and Sophie burst into fits of laughter and saw Jane standing at the door listening, tears running down her cheeks from laughter too. Pauline again grasped that a new era had started. This was the first time such laughter had filled the house, it was a good feeling. She felt glad for her Mum and renewed in herself. When they left Sophie remarked, "Your Mum is so happy Pauline, what a wonderful old bugger David is, fingers crossed she'll get out of here and start a new life."

During the day Pauline and Sophie cleaned up the house

and settled Sophie into her new room. Pauline observed that Sophie seemed to accept what had happened and in her own way wanted to get on with life, having mentioned many times that once her father passed on she would begin travelling again. She had found it a far more enjoyable way of life with no complications and if she got sick of a place she just moved on.

Pauline changed her mother's sheets aware the smell of sex still lingered in the room. It excited her. Even the nudge of Abdul's penis awakened her sensuality and deep down she wanted a full encounter. She had been highly aroused watching his penis become erect and ready to enter her. Actually Pauline was a little jealous of her mother's love life. She found David Anderson attractive, great company and so easy going, unlike her late father who never laughed or seemed happy, even when shafting Rita.

Pauline showered and set the table for four, eagerly awaiting her Mum and David's return, wondering what he would cook for dinner that evening. They arrived home about 5pm and unloaded several cartons onto the sink, both chatting happily about their day. An excited Jane informed them, "David has asked me to go back home with him and I have accepted. On Monday I will take the several months' leave I have accumulated and resign when that is finished."

"Mum, I am so happy for you and sure David will look after you." Pauline replied.

"I promise you that Pauline, your Mum is one special lady" said David beaming and unable to keep his hands off her.

Pauline also noticed her mother was more than happy to have her backside patted, idling up next to him, relishing each contact. 'Their behaviour was erotic, both priming each other ready for copulating on a grand scale', she mused.

Jane broke open cartons of beer and mixed drinks, 'leg openers' David called them, as all cracked cans laughing and talking at once about the day they had enjoyed.

"Okay folks, lead me to the barbie" David instructed, lifting the biggest steaks out of a box all three had ever seen.

"Sorry love no barbie at this house, we will have to use the frypan" Jane informed him.

"Shit really, no probs, frypan it will be, have you a couple?" David asked.

"Yep, I have one" Sophie chipped in, already onto her second can of Bundy, "it's in the garage, I'll get it."

By the time Pauline returned the pan was sizzling and, plonking hers on the stove, she noted even at this early hour, her mother and Sophie had popped their third can of Bundy. Pauline was sipping a beer with David, helping him peel onions and slicing tomatoes. Everyone was excited as the aroma of steak filled the kitchen. Cracking her second can for the first time ever, Pauline relaxed, surveying the scene. It was almost unreal how a home could change so dramatically in such a short time. Sunday night was always pizza night. Her late father would have had a fit. If he had ever seen these goings-on in his house she was sure he would have had a heart attack.

Jane was smiling and happy, onto her fourth drink,

more than she had consumed in one sitting in her life. It was slowly taking effect as she watched David turning great steaks in the pan, 'enough' she thought 'for everyone to live on for a month'. She was deliriously happy and feeling warm and sexy. It was nice to be wanted 'and the intimacy', she mused, was fabulous. Raising her glass she purred, "Here is to my next life with my fabulous lover. Girls he is a real 'bull' I can tell you, a one-hour-turnaround, what a man!"

David blushed, "Ah but Jane, a good bull needs a good heifer to be able to perform well with, and you are the best."

Jane was so overcome being heaped with such praise for the first time in her life that she swooned towards David embracing him as her hand rubbed his crotch.

"Sorry girls," he said passing the tongs to Pauline "Duty before food."

Grabbing Jane they dragged each other to the bedroom not even bothering to close the door. Pauline and Sophie watched in awe as clothes were shed everywhere. The alcohol having destroyed all her inhibitions, they soon heard loud moans from Jane. She was now a raving, lust machine.

Placing two steaks in the fridge the girls decided to share the other one. It was hard to concentrate as both sat listening to the shattering orgasm Jane was having, the sounds of lovemaking causing Pauline to swell in excitement. She knew she wanted what her mother was having and sooner rather than later.

"Your Mum is getting what most women want, if they

41

were being honest" said Sophie and, looking earnestly at Pauline continued, "one day I hope we both find a stud like David". I was thinking, in a few months' time, perhaps we could have a road trip and go up and visit them. Who knows, we might get laid on the way".

"Do you really think we could do that Sophie, how about work?" Pauline responded.

"Well Pauline, you can take your long service leave, I know you are owed heaps and I can pay off my debts to you and your Mum in three months, so in say five months we would be in a position to go." Sophie replied.

"Bloody hell Sophie, I will trade my car and buy us a campervan. To be honest the last few months have changed my life, I now want to live life. True what you say, I need a man bad Sophie. Never had a fuck but just to listen to my own bloody mother shagging makes me want some too" Pauline replied blushing.

"Are you serious Pauline, never had a good shag?" Sophie asked.

"Don't rub it in Sophie, never thought I was attractive to men but when that shit Abdul tried to get into me I somehow figured I might be more attractive to men than I thought, never really gave it a try. Actually my life, like Mum's, has been so boring" Pauline, now half pissed and sobbing, answered.

Sophie embraced her friend, "You are not only attractive Pauline but one of the nicest and most genuine people I have ever met. Promise me girl, we will go and have an adventure." "Promise" swore Pauline, through the alcoholic haze and approaching headache as Sophie helped her to her bedroom. This was her quest, her new direction.

Somehow she felt exhausted. Confessing to Sophie had drained her. She no longer felt in charge but vulnerable. She needed someone to want her as David wanted her mother and she swore to return that want with great gusto just as her mother had.

Chapter Five

Pauline woke to find her mother sitting on the bed with a glass of water in her hand and two Panadol, "Here have a good drink and take these. I actually feel a bit ashamed of leading my daughter astray" Jane said eyeing Pauline with a look only a mother could give.

Sitting up in bed Pauline replied, "Not really Mum, never had so much fun in my life and I am thirty six soon. I wish you had led me astray years ago, last night was a hoot!"

"I know I am being a bit hasty perhaps, but for the first time in my life I am deliriously happy. David is a bit short on detail, not sure where we are going to live. Possibly on some isolated station miles from nowhere but at my age the reality is that this might be my last chance in life to be truly happy. I am reasonably well off but David has never asked me about money and when we booked he seemed quite upset when I went to pay for my fare. He told me he was a bit old fashioned and felt a man should provide for his woman and from here on he would pay, so I guess he is not after my money" Jane told Pauline.

"Mum, perhaps the old saying is true, 'if you never, never go, you will never, never know' and it has taken me all these years to appreciate that there is a big country out there. My view is 'go you lucky bugger, live life to the full'. Sophie and I are coming up by road when you settle in, on my first big adventure. Unsure Mum what I am looking for but maybe a bit of loving and to broaden my vision. Actually I have to thank Sophie for that. All I know is that I don't want to spend my life doing the same thing every day until I die" Pauline told her mother decidedly.

Never one before to show emotion, Jane hugged Pauline with a tear rolling down her cheek. "We all make mistakes Pauline and mine was staying with your father. I knew he was shagging prostitutes on his trips but I was too weak to do anything about it. Now I know just how shit my life was and feel free, the shackles have been lifted. Yes, I may be making a big mistake but I can always come back here and to my job. I have three months to find out."

"Mum, go for it. I have never seen you so happy and I really like my 'new mother'. I can't believe how someone can change so quickly. Somehow I feel a new era is coming for us all including Sophie" Pauline replied.

"Oh well off to work I go, for the last day hopefully. If they object to me leaving without adequate notice I will get a doctor's certificate stating I am having a breakdown due to my husband's death, or something like that. One thing is for sure, come tomorrow morning 'Jane is on the plane'!" Jane laughed.

"I am not feeling too bad now Mum so off to work I go too, see you tonight" Pauline said jumping out of bed and heading to the shower. Sophie had gone already. In her job she was unable to work the flexible hours Jane and Pauline enjoyed.

Gulping down her coffee, Pauline chatted to her mother, "David, still in bed, Mum?"

"Yep he is having a day's rest here, he is still sleeping. I hope to be home early to pack." Jane informed her.

"Hope you haven't worn him out Mum!" Pauline joked.

"No such thing!" Jane laughed, "See you tonight, perhaps the last night in this house." Scooping up her mobile phone she headed for her car.

"Wait Mum, I will leave my car for David and come with you. I'll leave a note with the keys" Pauline shot back.

"Thanks Pauline, he may want to get out of the house for a break" Jane replied.

Both left, leaving the house unlocked and the slumbering David, heading to what Jane hoped was her last day after nearly four decades of working as a public servant. She would have retired anyhow in two years.

Pauline met Sophie as usual for coffee but somehow all the gossip now seemed to have lost its attraction, just a lot of self-centred people living in a fool's paradise of spin, manipulation and lies. The whole system existing in a world of unreality, decisions made to obtain votes despite the constant bleating of doing the best for 'Orstralia'.

Even in the bureaucracy loyalties and beliefs changed like the wind depending on what political persuasion was in power at the time. People she knew who had so called 'convictions' on many subjects nodded like maniacs for the cameras behind politicians ranting on against the very ideas they held so closely. Like sails in the wind, changing course to suit the moment and to further their careers.

Pauline also considered the present government she was serving was the worst in her time working as a public servant. Members, dancing around, hands waving in front of the press, never confronting a question but side-stepping and ranting on, blaming anyone and everything other than their own incompetence. The whole atmosphere was spiralling out of control, as was the debt no one wanted to hear about or confront but she knew Australia, like all countries, would one day have to pay it back.

Of all the people Pauline knew, Sophie had a greater awareness and vision than those trapped in a cocoon of self-interest and greed.

Pauline had a great inner sense of wanting to get away from it all and envied her mother for having the fortitude to follow her feelings, enjoy her new found sensuality and dare to live her dream.

"Come on Pauline don't go getting morbid on me. Keep the faith, three months and we are off into the wilds of real Australia. Watch your back, keep your head down!" Sophie laughed, as she gave a wave heading back to her message delivering. Pauline smiled back, she actually agreed with her, a girl who had burst into her life only a few short months ago.

Because this was possibly her mother's last day with her in this house, tonight she was going to make it a happy one for all. She decided to spend the day getting a few supplies for a farewell feast and 'yes' some more booze. Pauline decided then and there that this would also be a celebration of her new life, a change, a new direction. 'The new Pauline', a phrase she now heard often, was getting on with her life.

Returning to her office she packed up her desk and

informed a bored woman sitting next to her, playing on the computer, that she had a few meetings to attend. Walking from the building amid a throng of other people, Pauline headed for the beauty parlour. Yes, this was the start of the new Pauline, a vibrant and sexually liberated, living sex siren.

Then a visit to her local GP who gulped when Pauline informed her she wanted to go on the pill and also sought advice on a suitable diet. At first shocked, but warming to Pauline's new found want of a fitter and obviously sexual life, the GP advised her on healthy eating and exercise.

Next, Pauline spent more on clothing than she had done for years, buying fashionable, quite revealing clothes and new high heels. Already she was feeling liberated and it showed. All those she dealt with that day thought her an 'outgoing, vibrant young woman'.

Pauline purchased the most revealing underwear, lacy and sexy. Even trying it on made her feel racy just as the lacy teddy she had worn for the Abdul meeting had made her feel empowered. 'Yes' she mused, 'a few kilos off and this chick will be ready!' Her goal was to be fit and healthy before she and Sophie set off on their 'conquest' of Australia.

That evening even her own mother found it hard to believe the mindset and direction the new Pauline had set out on. Sophie too was amazed at the new Pauline, she and David were telling the most racy jokes.

Laughter and giggling vibrated throughout the house. Sophie thought the Police may even be called to this quiet street with such a rowdy party in progress. No one went to bed until after midnight, and then crashed exhausted, aching all over from laughter.

Pauline and Sophie waved a fond farewell to David who was looking a bit seedy and to a beaming Jane, setting off on a big adventure with her new lover, as excited as a teenager living the dream.

To Sophie's surprise Pauline drove home and parked the car in the drive. Hopping out, she picked up two bottles of water, "Come on Sophie old girl, our new life has begun. We are walking to work!"

"Fuck Pauline, it's an hour's walk" Sophie exclaimed.

"I know Sophie and we will walk home to a meal of salad. No more cakes or sweets until we are fit and I lose fifteen kilos" Pauline replied.

Sophie smiled, she knew Pauline was determined and was grateful to her and Jane for helping in her hour of need. If Pauline was going to do it, so was she and so began a health regime the envy of all those who knew them.

Pauline's concern for her Mum crumbled with a cheerful phone call from Jane on the second night after her departure. Basically, David did own a station but his son ran it. He was also heavily involved in other business ventures and owned homes in Darwin and Broome. David had taken her that afternoon to a car dealer and purchased her a new car.

At the time she phoned, Jane was overlooking Fanny Bay, appropriately named she mused, sitting on the balcony sipping a Bundy and Coke. Pauline knew by her Mum's voice she had landed in heaven. Sophie grabbed the

49

phone and made Jane repeat it all.

Both girls sat sipping water, now more than ever determined to break out and follow their dreams. The regime of getting fit had reached a new stage and buoyed by Jane's news both walked morning and night to work but extended the walk gradually after four weeks jogging to work in shorts and jogging shoes, changing at work. Pauline threw all her old dresses out replacing them with jeans and short skirts. The new Pauline was slowly rising from the ashes of the old Pauline. Now she was even oblivious to her surroundings and the constant politicking around her.

Following her mother's reports of her glamorous new lifestyle and sexual exploits that seemed to get more outlandish as time went on, the new Pauline was on a mission. So much so, one night when they arrived home after a marathon run, a new Winnebago was sitting in the drive. Pauline walked to the back of the house and returned with some keys, showing a gob-smacked Sophie the escape machine she had just had delivered.

No longer did the duo even discuss the day to day goings on in the national Capital even though it had turned into a circus. Instead the fitness regime and the new escape machine occupied every minute of their day. Planning the route and stocking the Winnebago kept them both excited and enthralled. That, along with Jane's day to day reports of helicopter rides, cattle mustering and dinner parties, made the mundane duties of work simply a necessary sideline to other more exciting duties.

Pauline lost twenty four kilos and decided the

transformation was complete. She now looked fantastic and Sophie warned her against going too far. They decided not to tell Jane or send photos. They wanted this to be a big surprise when the new Pauline swept back into her life.

Both girls were getting wolf whistles from work sites and admiring glances from passers-by but because of the fitness regime had not had any chance of meeting partners. Now it was time they decided to show their wares and have a girls' night out.

Seated at the bar having a quiet drink, they considered going home early. It seemed only couples were present and certainly no eligible bachelors, until two younger men from the local rugby club dropped in. They too seemed to be on the prowl and smiled at the girls several times, finally approaching and asking to join them.

A couple of hours passed and the younger one showed interest in Pauline. By now well primed, his hands began to wander. She had decided to give him a good ride, long before he whispered in her ear asking if she was interested in going back to his motel room!

She crossed the road and into the motel, knowing Sophie and her partner had already entered the room next door. Pauline was more than ready, now thirty six she was hogging for sex so much her pants had been soaking wet at the bar. Closing the door they became locked in a passionate embrace as her hands slipped down feeling for his penis. Grabbing hold of it she thought it seemed small, but lust drove her now.

Standing apart panting, they both undressed, Pauline's hungry eyes looking for the penis that was going to deflower her and begin her erotic journey to sexual nirvana. Pushing her towards the bed she opened her legs, breathing heavily in expectation as she felt him enter her - or had he, then she gathered that he was so small she had hardly felt anything. So swollen and ready was she, Pauline was disappointed when after three small thrusts he withdrew. She watched little spurts of semen shoot over her throbbing vagina, leaving her still hogging for a good shag.

Without speaking, his lust gone, he dressed as quickly as he had undressed and was on his way. Going to the bathroom, with her sexual desire waning and feeling deflated, Pauline dressed after cleaning herself up. Well, she decided, at least finally she'd had a cock in her. Although small it was still classed as a cock and she'd had semen discharged because of her sex appeal.

Sophie knocked on the door, her tale was as bad. Her man had failed to even get it up and had fallen asleep. Hailing a taxi both laughed like maniacs, sharing the big night of sexual adventure. 'Things can only improve' Sophie mused.

It was then, having a late night Milo, both decided to leave at the end on the month on their much needed big adventure. Pauline decided to just lock the house up. Their next door neighbours, now retired, had already promised to keep an eye on it until they returned.

Two weeks passed and Sophie received the sad news her father had passed away. She somehow felt no great sadness as he had hated his life in the home, although Sophie visited him three times a week. She knew he had lost his will to live and he just stared out the window. As she sat with him she often wondered what he was thinking. Perhaps, 'of good times passed' she hoped.

Pauline and Sophie were the only ones who attended the funeral. Sophie confided that they had no other relatives and with her father gone, she was now on her own.

Pauline looked at Sophie, "You will always be my friend Sophie. In fact you are my first real friend. Maybe now is the time for us both to start a new life."

Sophie laughed, "You know Dad told me before he died that we had both made bad choices in partners but at least he had a lucky strike with Mum. Maybe there is someone out there for us Pauline, so let's put it out there but if there is no one, let's go for a bit of loving anyway!"

Chapter Six

On a bleak and freezing Canberra morning the Winnebago pulled out with frost dancing in the headlights. Both Pauline and Sophie had been too excited and in high expectation to sleep that night. Now just breaking daylight with Sophie driving they headed west to Adelaide beginning a new adventure, planned for several months.

Jane was happy to hear her daughter was on the way. She had resigned when her long service leave had been used up, swearing to never visit Canberra again. She told the girls she didn't want to be reminded of her shit life, now in the past and never to return.

Progress was slow, dark cloud and freezing temperatures continued as they headed towards Echuca, their first planned overnight stay.

"How do you feel leaving Canberra?" Sophie struck up a conversation.

"Strange actually Sophie, at my age it seems surreal. I lived there all my life and I suppose if Dad were alive I would still be there" Pauline answered.

"So would your mother I suppose, your dad was some control freak" Sophie replied.

"You know Sophie I woke up, a few weeks back after he died, to what power he held over us, especially Mum. Her life was absolute shit and mine, no better" Pauline responded.

"I am a fine one to talk. We all think we know that

what we are doing is right but some men are manipulating, even cruel. From what your Mum said, your Dad kept her under his control with an iron fist while screwing other women. Strange, he had a hot chick in his bed but chose to make her suffer. My Dad was right, those kinds of men will never change but in most cases the women will even go back for more abuse and control in the mistaken belief that they will change" said Sophie thoughtfully looking at Pauline.

"True about Mum, wow can you believe her when the shackles came off. Never heard her swear in my life but now she has gone in the opposite direction, gone completely feral" Pauline laughed.

"Come on Pauline, your Mum is getting what all women want after all these years, be happy for her. I bet all those frustrated old prunes we worked with would love a strong man to sweep them off their feet and give them a good shagging" Sophie laughed, the atmosphere now changing, both eager to start a new chapter in their lives.

"I have made up my mind Sophie. If I have the luck to find a good man who wants to bed me for what I am and we have a sharing relationship, I intend like Mum to give him the best time ever in the cot, otherwise we will fuck for mutual satisfaction then move on. No mind games, abusive behaviour or manipulation for Pauline" Pauline informed Sophie.

"I'm with you Pauline. Next time for Sophie the man will keep me or fuck off" Sophie laughed.

"Hope we run into some good weather, sick of the cold, never liked it although I have lived all those winters in

Canberra" Pauline chatted.

"Possibly we will not get much really good weather until we get north of Perth in WA, dry season up north so I'm looking forward to seeing some blue sky. One thing, we will not have thousands of grey nomads on the Great Ocean Road, at Eyre, on the York Peninsula or crossing the Nullarbor" Sophie told Pauline.

"I am so glad you are with me Sophie, would never even consider this without you, it sounds so exciting. What the hell are grey nomads?" Pauline enquired.

"They are thousands of old retirees caravanning around the country, enjoying life. Wonderful lot they are too, having a ball and spending heaps on Viagra" Sophie laughed.

"All a dream, perhaps now I understand Mum. My shackles are off, all inhibitions gone and ready for anything Sophie, even going nude on Cable Beach like you told me" Pauline giggled.

"Hang on for the ride Pauline. Believe me, with me as your guide, all is possible" Sophie promised.

Several times they stopped to stretch their legs and enjoy a coffee, and make a sandwich from the well-stocked larder in their new mobile home. It was dusk when the tired travellers pulled into a caravan park, surprised that only seven fellow travellers occupied the park.

"I thought we may have to book ahead, where are the tourists?" Pauline asked the lady behind the desk in the office.

"Up north lovey, this is our quiet season. The oldies, lucky buggers are enjoying the sun, not freezing their arses off here" the office lady replied passing them keys to the amenities.

Pauline watched as Sophie backed into a spot and both set up the water and power connections under Sophie's direction. Pauline was intrigued and set out to explore the amenities in the park. Even though their Winnebago had a toilet and shower, Sophie had recommended using park facilities when they could and to keep the Winnebago's facilities for off road camping.

Several times they stopped and chatted to fellow campers, most seemed to be heading north for the winter. Two stated they usually left earlier than this but commitments had held them up. One young man on his own from Tasmania was heading to Queensland to work in the mines and accepted an invitation to come over for drinks after he finished his meal.

Sophie and Pauline admitted they both felt tired. The previous evening's excitement at leaving had kept them awake and they had little sleep. They broke open a bottle of wine to celebrate their first night on the road and after two glasses were quite relaxed so decided to shower and change for bed. Returning from the showers wrapped in dressing gowns they saw their guest waiting with a couple of bottles under his arm. They looked at each other both realising they had forgotten the invitation but smiled and invited their guest in.

The heater had made the Winnebago warm and inviting as they sat around the table swapping yarns and both sides told their story as to why they were on the road. The young Tasmanian had lost his job in the forestry like hundreds in Tasmania and his only show of finding a job was to head to the mines.

Two bottles of wine later Pauline could see Sophie was getting more than a little interested in their visitor.

"Gee it's warm in here" she purred, standing up and slipping the robe off showing her sheer nighty and perky breasts.

The visitor gulped and sipped at his wine. Pauline saw the bulge under the table nearly bursting out of his trousers. Winking at Sophie she also slid her dressing gown off to expose two large ripe breasts and, if he were to look below, a wet pussy.

"Girls, have to be honest," the ready to roll guest croaked, "like to have a go but which one? Don't want to cause friction."

"Fuck us both big boy, we don't mind and we like a bit of friction!" Sophie teased, sliding her panties off ready for action. Pauline followed suit, then they removed their tops and both stood naked before a gob-smacked guest.

The girls approached him and slowly removing his clothing, directed him to the queen size bed. Sophie, leading him by his erect penis, pushed him onto the bed.

Maneuvering him into the middle of the bed, Sophie sucked on his penis as Pauline kissed him, placing his trembling hands onto her voluptuous breasts.

Sophie tapped Pauline on the back gently and seeing her dripping pussy pointed to the wet, shining, throbbing cock. Pauline needed no persuasion and straddling it gave a deep gasp as she impaled herself on the first cock to stretch her vagina. Shuddering and moaning with pleasure she slowly rose up and down meeting each thrust as her lover now grabbing her arse pumped in ecstasy. Sophie guided his fingers into her dripping vagina transfixed by the cock pumping in and out of Pauline's soaking pussy. Pauline looked into his glazed eyes as he shuddered and she felt the hot spunk coming from his swollen member, disappointed as she felt it slip from her. She had enjoyed the experience and knowing Sophie had watched his cock ream in and out of her was exciting but she knew the moment was far too quick and her rising fire had not reached its potential but the elation of knowing she had been properly fucked stimulated her senses.

Sophie sucked hungrily on the flaccid penis while Pauline tickled his balls at Sophie's goading, both hungry for more. As the penis slowly stiffened Sophie mounted and, fully aroused, plunged wildly, coming in an earth shattering climax which Pauline now understood was the ultimate peak a woman can reach and, as Sophie had informed her, was the nirvana of a good fuck.

Sophie's body was shuddering. Pauline fascinated, eyes transfixed as she fingered herself, stared at Sophie's swollen vagina dripping wet, slowly slid up and down enjoying the sensation in the afterglow of orgasm.

Sophie with eyes glazed saw Pauline rubbing her vagina and sliding off looked at Pauline pointing to the still erect penis. Pauline again mounted and unable to control herself, now so swollen and excited, plunged madly consuming the cock deep within her. Unable to control the coming torrent, her body shuddered and she gasped in pleasure as waves of sperm again shot into her, but this time she climaxed. Soaking in sweat she collapsed onto the bed. Pauline had made it, at thirty seven she had orgasmed.

No one spoke for a long time. Their exhausted lover was now asleep and so was Sophie. Pauline too, unable to keep her eyes open, dozed off.

During the night Pauline was woken by her legs being parted. Still half asleep she felt the penis enter her and instantly placed her arms around her lover, pulling her legs up she gave small gasps as she felt her vagina fill with his throbbing penis. Slowly he rose in out, completely withdrawing before thrusting deep into her, each thrust bringing a shudder from Pauline. As she wrapped her legs around his body she knew he was playing with her, withdrawing and making her beg for more until, after what seemed an eternity, he thrust deep into her riding her like a raging bull, the bed bouncing up and down. Again Pauline felt the climax coming and loudly begged him to fuck her harder. She felt a torrent gushing from her, wetting the sheet as she reached another orgasm. Just as she felt him come again deep inside her he collapsed on her, soaked in sweat and breathing heavily, his mouth seeking hers in a deep kiss.

He rolled off her but Pauline was too exhausted to get off the bed so instead, lay her leg over him in a deep afterglow, her wanting had been quenched.

Pauline heard as daylight broke Sophie groaning and begging for more as she had done but Pauline was too exhausted, sinking contentedly into the sheets with a smile on her face, it had been a special night, both had shared sexual gratification. Now it was not talk, Pauline had for the first time without reservation let herself reach the ultimate pleasure, no ties or promises made, her lust just satisfied - a new era had indeed commenced.

When Pauline did finally wake up she could smell coffee. Surprised, she saw their love, whose name she had now forgotten, with Sophie, both dressed and watching the news on TV, enjoying breakfast.

"Hi sleepy head" Sophie laughed.

"What time is it?" Pauline replied yawning.

"Eight o'clock, Mark has to leave, he is on a time schedule" Sophie said.

"Yep, worst luck, thanks to both of you for a wonderful time. Honestly, most men would only dream about what we had and I really needed it. I was a bit down actually, so thanks heaps," Mark told them "hope one day we can catch up again."

"Tell you what Mark, if all my future roots are as good as that I will have no complaints" Pauline chuckled.

Mark kissed them both and they parted friends. He had even told Sophie she informed Pauline later, that he was married and going ahead to hopefully find work to start a new life.

"Actually I guessed so but we did him no harm" Pauline said in response to the news, "I suppose our fleeting meeting cheered the poor guy up and we were not trying to take him from his wife."

It would be nearly midday before they left the park. Having showered they washed the sheets and dried them in the dryer. Pulling out onto the highway they now agreed to slow down, bugger a time frame, they would enjoy themselves and forget schedules.

"Tell you one thing Pauline that was a good night. Sex should be enjoyed, even shared as we did. All the taboo about sex is bullshit, it is a big part of the human agenda and we should express our sexuality more honestly and openly" Sophie said smiling.

"Well that seemed natural to me. The three of us enjoyed the encounter and actually it was a turn on seeing you get humped" Pauline laughed.

"Have to admit it was better than a porno watching you get it off too. I was so bloody horny I came like a steam train when I got my turn, I was soaking wet" Sophie grinned.

"Down to whatever you are comfortable with really. To me it was just sex, so saw no harm in it but have we raised the benchmark too high?" Pauline quipped, "Old Mark was good. I envy his wife!"

"Possibly, although like he said, it is many a man's dream to shag two women hogging for it so we did turn him on and alcohol relaxes, sometimes letting the real emotions come out" confided Sophie.

Chapter Seven

Over the next couple of weeks the duo became even more relaxed and settled into a routine of sharing the driving. A new world opened up for Pauline. Canberra had been the centre of her world. Never had she even dreamt how big Australia was, now becoming aware of the millions of Australians living their lives controlled by the ambitions of those who grasped for power, so far removed from the real Australia she now drove through.

Several times they camped out by rivers and beaches, most evenings joined by friendly older travellers, and many an evening they sat enjoying wonderful conversation over a few drinks as the sun set. It was by way of these conversations that Pauline began to grasp the disgust most felt towards Canberra and political parties. Because of the hostility of many they met, both she and Sophie decided not to mention that they actually worked in the public service!

Several times laying in bed they alluded to the meeting with 'Tassie' as they had nicknamed Mark, the man with whom they had both spent such an erotic interlude. Just the conversation, they admitted and thoughts of the encounter, made them feel horny.

It was when they reached Streaky Bay in South Australia while walking from the caravan park on the beach to the local hotel for an evening meal that they pondered their chances of getting some more action. The thoughts they whispered to each other arose the sexual feelings in both and each considered when they sat down for the meal that, perhaps if they played their cards right, the three men drinking at the bar and glancing at them, may make their evening very interesting.

As they finished the meal and a bottle of wine one of the admirers sauntered over and introduced himself.

"Hi girls, I'm Ivan from Adelaide. We are here working on the Jetty, feel like a drink?" he asked.

"Sophie and Pauline, travelling to WA, don't mind if we do" Sophie replied.

Joining the group, they chatted about various things, enjoying the company. They excused themselves and went to the toilet both waiting while the other did a pee. Washing their hands both straightened their hair and Sophie said, "Well will we fuck em or not, better to be honest than sit there all night, I can tell they want us, are you game?"

"Take on all three?" Pauline gulped.

"Look Pauline, we are not after a long-term gig with these guys just a good fuck, no use sitting there with dripping fannies" Sophie grinned.

"Okay, if I went home now I wouldn't sleep. Yep to be honest, after Tassie, I need a good shagging" Pauline decided.

"Look, these guys are possibly all married and looking for some fun so let us set the agenda and the rules straight up" Sophie suggested.

Making their way back to the bar they both stood together and Sophie looked straight at the three smiling faces.

"Look boys, let's cut the bullshit and save time or we could be sitting here for hours listening to you trying to chat us up. We are both willing to fuck the three of you but no rough play and use condoms. If you try anything or no condoms we will leave. You're probably all married and just want a bit on the side so hope you don't disappoint us and can satisfy our wants too" Sophie told the three stunned men.

"Well to be honest we discussed who of us was going to try for you both but now no decision, let's go to our room and we will show you we can satisfy you both" Ivan the spokesman replied rearing to go.

The five retreated to the bedroom of two of them, two single beds. All, knowing what was happening, got naked and Pauline guided Ivan to the bed. Slipping a condom on him she leant over giving him a head job as did Sophie with one of the others.

Pauline was taken by surprise when the third member entered her from behind and slowly rammed in and out of her swelling pussy as she slipped her lips up and down Ivan's throbbing cock. Pauline glanced over at Sophie, glad she had not taken on her stud. His cock was huge and Sophie groaned now as he held her legs apart reaming in and out of her, his eyes transfixed on his cock and her vagina. Picking up speed and slapping his huge balls on her wet buttocks, Sophie moaned even louder.

Pauline felt her fuck buddy shudder, disappointed he'd come too fast. Straddling Ivan she rode him pounding up and down feeling her rising fire but was again disappointed when he groaned and she knew he was ejaculating.

Sliding off she saw both men removing full condoms, watching in awe as Sophie, jerking spasmodically, reached an orgasm as did her rider, his big dick slipping out of her gaping vagina.

They sat gaining their composure each drinking a can of cold beer. Strange, like old friends, the rules had been set and all complied. This was to be a sex session where all hoped to get satisfaction.

Pauline sat next to Sophie's partner with the big cock, it intrigued her and a tingling sensation went through her body. Only shagging him would satisfy her so, leaning down she began to suck on the slack cock and following Sophie's lead, ran her fingers up and down tickling the head while he fingered her dripping pussy. Pauline watched Sophie riding Ivan while giving their spare lover a head job and by the time her lover came up she was ready. He dragged her up doggy fashion and more than ready she pushed her buttocks back to assist the monster entering her. Crying out in gasps of pain and pleasure Pauline at last began to shudder, wanting more as he drove deep into her and picking up his pace she heard the squishing sound of her wetness as his huge balls rammed against her with each thrust.

Pauline knew her orgasm was approaching but it was different to what she had so far experienced, she felt weak now as spurts of juice came from her. She had heard of female ejaculation and realised she was experiencing it now, so strong was her orgasm she nearly blacked out. Her lover continued to plough in and out and she now so wet and swollen cried for more. Insatiable now, only extended and hard sex would satisfy her. Pauline looked behind, through her misty eyes she saw her rider was sweating, it was dripping from him, his face was grimacing as he moaned loudly and she felt him slowly stop. As he ejaculated she felt the semen hit her and knew at once that the condom had come off during the sexual act, which she calculated had lasted a little over an hour.

Sophie was seated with the other two and Pauline knew by the look on her face that she too was satisfied. Pauline got to her feet helped by the big-cock shagger. Staggering to the bathroom she sat on the toilet trying to fish the condom out but had no success so went back to the room.

"Thanks girls, you two are remarkable, in all my life this has been the best session I have had. No pretense, we all knew what we wanted, saved hours' of bullshit. Hope we satisfied you both."

"I agree, better to put your cards on the table. If all parties in a sex session were honest it would be so much better. Honestly, we all knew what we wanted and 'yes' boys, especially big boy, complete satisfaction. Now, who has slim fingers, I have a condom to fish out?" Pauline giggled.

"Big dick, small slim fingers" her big boy smiled, and seated on the bed he gently ran a long finger into her, pulling the condom out.

Dressing, the duo set off back to the caravan park. The night was fine and as they walked past the fence towards the park entrance Sophie giggled. "Tell you what Pauline big boy certainly knew how to fuck, that was the best root

I have ever had."

Pauline chuckled, "I certainly enjoyed it and to be honest really needed it, weeks without sex I am finding hard to accept."

The two did not see an old chap on the opposite side of the fence sitting under his annexe.

"Tell you what girls, wish I was younger and more attractive. Love to take you both on."

Both burst into laughter, "Cheeky Bugger" Sophie replied.

"After what we just had old timer, don't think you'd make the grade" Pauline joined in.

"Bill, here girls. Don't put old men down, never judge until you know what you're talking about" Bill shot back.

"Okay Bill, we will call in for a nightcap" Sophie replied as they walked on.

"Do you mean that Sophie?" Pauline asked alarmed.

"Why not, the old codger is lonely so let's make his day, we both reek of sex, one drink won't harm us" she replied.

Inside the park they soon found Bill still quietly sitting under his annexe. A small light shone on his face and they were both shocked, he was really good looking, well-built and had the kindest, most relaxing smile. They sat down in the two chairs he had made ready.

"Apologies girls, never meant to seem crude. I was just amused at your banter with each other, sounds as if you had a good night. By the way my name is Bill Williams" Bill introduced himself.

"Sophie and Pauline," Pauline informed him "actually

we should apologise also. We sounded like real tarts but are only two frustrated women unable to get a steady man in our lives, so chose to get laid. Actually Bill, I was a virgin a year ago."

"No shame Pauline, at least you are honest. Strange, sadly I lost my wife a year ago and 'yes' we all need sex or, if we are truthful, we do. I can't judge anyone, when I picked up my new caravan in Adelaide I spent several nights with prostitutes" Bill replied.

"Really, there are heaps of women about of your age Bill. How old are you anyway? Sophie questioned.

"Like you girls, hard to find someone without problems or baggage. I am sixty one Sophie. Gets so lonely sometimes, it's hard to sleep when you've been used to someone in your bed. The fact is, sex slows down but it's the companionship and company you miss most" Bill told them.

The two chatted and enjoyed a relaxing drink with their new found friend, who they gleaned was off to Broome. He had worked there as a stock agent until his wife became ill and they moved to the Eyre Peninsula so she could get medical attention in Adelaide as and when required.

"Would you know David Anderson?" Pauline asked.

"Yep actually know him quite well. Have a house next to him in Cable Beach, known David for years. I believe he is on his own like me but we'll catch up on this trip, it's been a couple of years since I have been home" Bill replied.

"Really what a coincidence Bill, my mother is living with him and has been for a few months. That is why we are heading up there" Pauline replied in surprise.

"Well Pauline he is a wonderful chap, into cattle and mining. He has a son Ross who runs the cattle enterprise, which is struggling a bit at the moment because of those idiots in Canberra but luckily Bill is an astute business man and has a stake in several mining ventures" Bill informed them, now really interested as were both girls.

"Well seems like we will see each other again Bill, better try and get some sleep" Sophie said leaning over and giving their new friend a goodnight kiss. Pauline noticed Sophie, although twenty five years his junior hung on his every word and seemed to really like the easy going Bill.

"Yep I am off across the Nullarbor in the morning, will fuel up in Ceduna and camp at an off road site tomorrow evening" Bill replied getting up ready to leave.

"We might follow you Bill and see each other over the Nullarbor, perhaps camp at the same spot tomorrow night. We will cook you dinner" Sophie offered.

"Darn good idea. Actually, if one of us breaks down we will have backup" Bill responded enthusiastically.

"Done Bill, let's say a 7am start" Sophie suggested.

The sex had been fantastic and laying in bed Pauline felt tired. She understood now that, although starting late in life, she needed intimacy. In her deepest thoughts she longed for someone in her life like David Anderson.

"Night Sophie, Bill is a nice old chap, great to have him with us on the next leg" Pauline yawned.

"Bill might be old Pauline but in my experience at least a girl would know where he was each night, in bed next to you and he is a real gentleman" Sophie shot back.

"Sophie you like him, come on admit it" Pauline now awake replied.

"Pauline at my age the chance of finding some man really nice who would take care of me is so remote. I had jumped at the chance to marry Abdul knowing it was not going to work but didn't want to admit it. So to me a few years of bliss with someone who really loved me and took care of me would be better than nothing" Sophie replied sobbing.

Pauline sat up and held her friend, "I apologise Sophie. What you say is so true, sex for sex's sake is fine but in the end we all want someone to love and want us."

"To be honest Pauline I frightened myself tonight. Luckily you never saw me but I took on two at once and the frightening thing was I was loving it as you were, so I'm happy to admit it, I was so hot I was screaming for more and was actually sorry when they both came" Sophie confessed.

"I am guilty too Sophie, let my inhibitions completely go. I suppose alcohol helps but I just could not get enough and have been thinking seriously about myself. Is that what I want to turn into? It was actually a little frightening when I think back. If it had been ten men I would have still dragged them on! There just has to be more to good sex than that" Pauline soberly replied.

"Your mother has it all now. A man who brings her off and loves her for what she is plus look how he is taking care of her, Pauline! That is what we all want deep down. Tonight I turned into a raving tart and now I feel ashamed" Sophie sobbed.

"Unfortunately if one wants a good sex life we have not much choice, anyhow let's sleep, we have a big day tomorrow" Pauline replied turning off the light as the two friends cuddled into each other gaining strength from each other's presence.

Chapter Eight

A fine morning greeted them as they pulled out of the park. Bill was waiting and without fanfare pulled in behind the Winnebago with his four wheel drive and caravan.

Now with little traffic Pauline drove and was gaining confidence daily. They arrived at Ceduna mid-morning and after filling with fuel drove down to the wharf area to have morning tea. Bill supplied some fruit cake, his favourite he informed them, as they sat on a park bench looking at the tourists, although small in number, catching squid on the wharf.

"Sleep well last night girls? Bill asked, "I did after our little chat, it settled me down a bit" he added.

"Actually our consciences caught up with us Bill and we felt a bit ashamed of last night even though we both admitted we enjoyed it at the time" Sophie confessed.

"My dear Sophie and Pauline let me assure you both that we all do things we look back on with some shame, that's life. You are, in my opinion, two fine young women with a good life ahead so face to the wind, what is past is past. Let the one without sin cast the first stone" Bill remarked getting up and taking the two plastic coffee cups from the girls, throwing them in the garbage bin nearby.

"Thanks Bill, you are a gem!" Pauline replied.

"Please girls I am no better than you, I had it off with young prostitutes so I too have tinges of guilt but we three are better than many, at least we confess our guilt.

So let's just enjoy the drive across the mighty Nullarbor" Bill said smiling.

"Pauline, do you mind if I travel awhile with Bill, at least until lunchtime?" Sophie asked.

"By all means Sophie, you two go ahead and choose a spot for lunch. I will follow" Pauline replied happily.

"Are you sure girls, never meant to break you two up or impose?" Bill remarked.

"Bill we have been together since we left so a few hours apart won't be a problem, might save us killing each other" Pauline kidded.

Pauline waited and followed when Bill pulled out. She noticed the check point for incoming traffic and knew that on crossing the WA border they would have to declare any prohibited items. So for their dinner that evening they agreed to cook up all the vegetables they had left and Bill even suggested stopping well before dark so they had sufficient time to prepare.

Pauline appreciated her alone time, it gave her time to reflect. She had to admit she was enjoying her new found freedom and felt quite content. Despite her misgivings about their latest sexual adventure she secretly yearned for more now her sexuality had been awakened. She realised that after so many years of sexual frustration she needed intimacy. 'Perhaps' she mused, 'no more group sex but put herself out there and grasp an opportunity when and if it surfaced'.

Pauline was fascinated by the scope of her surroundings. Eagles feasting off numerous road kill, some getting killed themselves by the never ending stream of trucks crossing both ways in small convoys, often of three or four in line. Bill to her relief set a steady but safe pace. Even so she hung back a little to facilitate the passing of road trains, the drivers happily giving a toot as she pulled out as far as possible when she saw the road was clear ahead.

Pauline enjoyed the friendly waves of the truckies, some of whom she noticed were women, driving the big rigs. She became even more aware that her closeted life had been far different from that of the men and women who actually kept commerce going. Not stifling it with stupid laws designed to help but really making life harder, simply to appease the arrogance of those who did not have a clue how the real world she now moved in existed.

Even though she tried in her more reflective times to erase from her mind what happened in Streaky Bay, she felt rushes of sexual stirring below when she relived the wild thrusting and complete abandonment to pleasure she had enjoyed. Her thoughts made her wet and she knew going without sex for weeks was now not an option. She frowned as she foresaw the problem of satisfying her sexual awakening. She knew too that true happiness would only come to her, as it had come to her mother, by finding a partner as capable as David to quell and sate her desires.

About 1pm Bill stopped in a pull off under the shade of some low trees. Pauline, embarrassed when she noticed her shorts showed wet stains, changed before joining the others already setting up lunch in Bill's caravan. Sophie under Bill's directions seemed right at home cutting up tomatoes and cold meat from his fridge. Despite objections from both girls he insisted on supplying lunch but was happy for them to cook up all the vegetables, and use what fruit they had left, for the evening meal.

Pauline was surprised how comfortable and safe both felt in Bill's presence, as if they had known him for years. She noticed also that he seemed to have a calming effect on Sophie who enjoyed their banter and the age gap didn't seem that apparent. It was then that Pauline was convinced Sophie had indeed set her sights on Bill who of course was lapping up the attention after months of loneliness. Now with company he was in his element and 'yes' Pauline mused, 'our Sophie will bed you sooner than you think Bill, my dear man'!

Pauline decided to aid her friend and suggested that if he did not mind, perhaps Sophie might like to also spend the afternoon drive with Bill. She immediately saw in Bill's eyes a twinkle and he accepted subject to Sophie's consent. Sophie beaming said she had had a lovely morning with Bill and would love to.

Pauline was rather glad, after Sophie's constant chatter for the last few weeks it was nice to have one's own company for a few hours. She had actually enjoyed the morning's drive and now, as she looked around at the vastness of the Nullarbor, Pauline decided not to go back to her old life. A different world existed out here and she now understood why her mother grabbed the chance to leave Canberra. Pauline decided too that should an opportunity like Sophie was obviously going to go for happen, she, in her mother's own words, intended to give her man the best ever experience in bed, copulating with him so well, that he would be as infatuated with her as

David was with her mother. The thought somehow justified the sexual trysts she had experienced, how else was she to know what good sex was if one never experienced good sexual contact?

The afternoon floated by in a haze of wonderment at the scenery so vast and harsh yet enthralling to Pauline as she explored her inner most thoughts, finding it hard to believe she was cruising the Nullarbor in a large motor home. Only a couple of years ago her life was so regimented and sterile that if someone had suggested to her what had now transpired she would have scoffed at the idea.

Just as the sun was setting Bill and Sophie pulled into a parking area dotted with several other vans. Finding a sheltered spot Bill backed into it followed by Pauline. It was a beautiful site, quiet and away from the others. Both vans had showers and toilets plus deep cycle batteries for off road camping.

Pauline busied herself with preparing tea, now part of her daily routine and she enjoyed it as if a sense of normality had entered her life. Sophie showered and changed, Pauline noted, into shorts and top both revealing and applied some makeup. While Pauline showered Sophie watched the cooking and noticed happily that Bill had seated himself and was watching her. When Pauline had finished she stepped from the shower wrapped in a towel.

"Sorry Pauline I will leave while you change" Bill said.

"Stay here Bill you will see nothing more than you have seen before!" Pauline wisecracked, pulling up panties under the towel before dropping the towel and pulling on a shirt then shorts.

"You are part of the works now Bill so stop worrying, you can look at me anytime, you are a wonderful man" Sophie giggled.

"Old man's dream Sophie lovey, why lust after something you can never have?" Bill quizzed.

"Now Bill Williams, any woman would be proud to have you. Age means little, it is what is in the heart that counts" Sophie answered.

"Look Bill, the girl is telling you she wants you, okay! One thing I have learnt is to speak your feelings, life flies by, be honest Bill. Take her to your bed, she is yours if you want her" Pauline broke in.

"Are you serious Sophie I am over sixty for hell's sake" Bill swallowed hard.

"I told Pauline Bill that I'd rather have a decade with a man who wanted me than thirty years of hell with someone who abused me. I have no family and just need a man who loves me for what I am and will look after me" Sophie replied.

"You sure are honest Sophie and to be as honest, I really enjoyed your company this afternoon and am not going to turn down a chance to bed such a prize. Let's try it over the next couple of weeks on our way to Broome and you decide at the end if you want to formalise it" Bill suggested.

"Formalise, what do you mean Bill?" Sophie asked.

"Well if all works out Sophie, I have no family like you so let's get married then we will have each other and you will be okay when I die" Bill replied.

"Don't want your money Bill just someone who wants me for what I am and takes care of me," Sophie replied "but I will need a divorce" she added.

"I just cannot believe this is happening but then why waste your life wondering? Make a decision and at least give it a go, happiness is fleeting. I am sure you two will make a go of it" Pauline said looking at them both, amazed at how life can change in a second just by seizing the moment.

With the meal finished and the washing up done Sophie and Bill adjourned to his caravan. The lights went off shortly after. Pauline spent a long sleepless night wondering what was happening next door and about their haste but appreciated that life must be grabbed with both hands. Sophie and Bill had both been seeking something. She hoped for them the happiness her mother had found and one day hopefully she too would find. She sighed as she switched off the light.

Pauline was woken up by an excited Sophie packing her clothes, smiling like a cat coming from the dairy. "Come on Sophie give, what happened?" Pauline blurted.

"Well Pauline last night was fantastic. He's gentle and erotic, we fucked five times. I am in love for the first time in my life, what a man!" Sophie chirped.

"Oh that is just great Sophie. I will help you move your gear, but can we stick together until Broome?" Pauline queried.

"Of course Pauline, Bill insists we travel as a group. I will even give you a spell driving when you want. I'm grabbing this with both hands Pauline because I know

I have a real chance of finding lasting happiness" she replied. Pauline had never seen Sophie so happy and content and knew that if she hadn't been so gregarious and capable of living outside the square, none of this would have happened. Just as her mum Jane had seized her opportunity for happiness with David.

Bill came into the Winnebago and started to help pack Sophie's belongings. "Pauline I apologise to you for what I have done. If you like and Sophie agrees, she can go on with you to Broome and we can meet there. I really feel bad about what has happened although to be honest I am in heaven, just cannot believe my luck. Before I met you both I was a lost soul, never in my wildest dreams did I even consider I would find someone like Sophie, in fact both of you. Under all the bravado beats two beautiful hearts."

Pauline without hesitation replied, "Bill Williams you darling man, there is no way ever I would consider such a thing. Sophie's happiness and indeed yours is paramount to me. It makes me want to cry just seeing you two lost souls meet up and make each other so happy. To tag along is all I ask".

"Thank you Pauline, you will always be my best friend as you are Sophie's. I have to admit when I wake at night and feel Sophie next to me that my heart nearly explodes with happiness and I find it now impossible to even contemplate life without her" Bill gushed.

Sophie listened but said nothing and with small tears of happiness running down her cheeks she stopped to hug Pauline. Bill too was choked with emotion and somehow

Pauline knew these two, no matter what, would stand the test of time. "If only!" Pauline sighed.

Pauline, herself emotionally drained, pulled out onto the highway behind Bill and Sophie. For once she really missed her mother and decided as soon as she had phone signal to give her a call. Although she felt happy for Sophie she also felt as if she had lost her only true, real friend. She hadn't understood until now just how much she had relied on Sophie since their first meeting and the subsequent bonding of two lost souls in the wilderness. Pauline was deep in thought as continuing her new adventure she drove on into the west.

Twice that long day they stopped for breaks, snacking on cheese and biscuits. Sophie offered to drive on both occasions but somehow Pauline felt she needed to be alone. They decided to put the extra effort into finishing the journey and stay at Norseman that night. It was a tiring day and Pauline was glad when they finally pulled into the park. It was after 7pm.

When Pauline along with Bill and Sophie booked in she informed them she was going for a jog, she really felt like a run after having been driving for over 12 hours.

She needed milk so put a ten dollar note in her shirt pocket and changing into her runners decided to give her mother a call before she headed off.

Her mother answered promptly, "Hi Pauline I've been waiting for your call, where are you now love?"

"In Norseman Mum, made it to WA at last, how are you?"

"Fine, living the dream but really miss you. Been

thinking a lot about you of late, can't wait to see you. By the way how is our Sophie?" Jane enquired.

"God Mum you won't believe this story. Sophie is not travelling with me. Well, yes she is but I am following her and her new man and guess what, he has a house next door to David in Broome!" Pauline told her mother.

"You are kidding me! I am in Broome now, on one side is a married couple and on the other David told me is a Surgeon who recently lost his wife. She was ill for years and they moved to Adelaide so she had better treatment" Jane replied as Pauline heard her telling David in the background.

"Shit Mum, a Surgeon, you are kidding me right?" Pauline challenged.

"No. Is his name Bill Williams and is he about 60?" Jane now excited, asked.

"Bloody hell Mum, cannot believe any of this. I really don't think Sophie even knows that!" Pauline blurted out.

"Very nice chap David tells me, a true gentleman. David keeps an eye on his home here, it is lovely. They had an apartment in SA somewhere also and last time David heard from him he was buying a caravan and bringing his equipment back here. He hoped to go back to work at the hospital part time" Jane informed Pauline.

"Mum I am gob smacked, just thought he was some nice, honest, lonely older man but he held back about his profession" Pauline replied trying to come to terms with the news.

"David tells me he is like that and Sophie under her tough exterior is a lost soul Pauline, we are so happy for them both. David is going to have a get together when you all arrive. We have some news of our own too so travel safely and get here as soon as possible" Jane instructed.

"What news Mum?" Sophie asked

"A surprise for when you all arrive, one big celebration love" Jane informed Pauline.

"Okay Mum you bugger, I won't sleep tonight now with my mind in overload. Off for a long jog and then dinner with the new lovers" Pauline replied switching the phone off and trying to come to terms with Jane's information.

Leaving the park Pauline jogged towards the town centre feeling elated. With the cool breeze in her face and dusk beginning to settle she jogged over several blocks, only stopping to look at iron cutouts of camels set back from the main town square. The shop was closed but Pauline noticed the hotel was still open and feeling thirsty decided to go in for a quick drink.

Entering she noticed a woman behind the bar with huge breasts and bottle-blonde hair looking the worse for wear. Seated at the bar were two men, 'possibly truckies' she thought in shorts and singlets who hardly gave her a glance. Only one other man was drinking, he had long trousers on, several tattoos, was dirty and had no top on at all.

Pauline ordered a beer and without reply the barmaid plonked the drink on the counter, swept up the ten dollar note and returned with the change.

"Where ya from lovey?" the barmaid asked.

"Canberra, on my way to Broome" Pauline replied.

"Long trip for a woman, lovey. On your own are you?"

"No with two friends, just went for a jog before dinner."

"Better get going lovey, soon be totally dark. A few roughies round here, they'll soon take advantage of a lone woman" the barmaid informed her.

Pauline had no intention of staying anyway. Finishing her drink she stepped out into the night but failed to notice that the man who'd been alone had already left. As Pauline made her way to the main street with lights now twinkling along it she passed through the shade of a side street. She froze when she felt the presence of someone step from the shade and roughly pull her into the dark alley pushing her violently against the wall.

"Ya gonna get a fuck ya bitch so behave and I won't fucken bash ya brains out" a terrifying voice rasped, the smell of sweat and alcohol reeking from her attacker.

Petrified, Pauline felt weak as his hand roughly pushed down her shorts, tearing the fastener as he drove a finger into her vagina. In so much pain she almost fainted, her knees buckling and, unable to fight, she resigned herself to being raped or perhaps even killed.

"Let her go Trevor you sick fucking bastard, knew you was up to no fucking good you animal" Pauline heard recognising the barmaid's voice.

Pauline felt him releasing her and she dropped to the ground.

"Fuck off Margaret, you fucking moll or I'll fuck you too" the attacker screamed.

"Go ahead you weak bastard. I called the cops so it'll be back to prison, you rapist prick. Go home to your slut and her slut mother. Keep your pox in the family" the barmaid screamed helping Pauline to her feet as the attacker ran off at the news.

Her saviour the barmaid helped Pauline back to the hotel. A traumatised Pauline twice vomited, her head throbbed.

"Margaret is my name, lovey. I will get my car and take you home. Frankly I didn't call the cops. To be honest the court case would be as bad as the attack, fucken lawyers would portray you as a slut asking for it! He has just done nine years for rape, I'll have a quiet word to the local coppers and they will handle the bastard" Margaret told Pauline.

Pauline remembers Margaret helping her into the car. Pushing open the pub door as they passed to the rear car park Margaret yelled, "Jacko take care of the bar for a while mate please, no free fucken beers neither, see ya shortly."

Although she knew it was wrong not to report the attempted rape as the attacker would likely offend again, Pauline heeded Margaret's advice and decided not to do so. Reliving the event in Court perhaps several times was not something she wished to do.

Regaining some composure Pauline looked at her saviour. "Thanks Margaret, he would have killed me, how can I ever repay you?" she asked, voice shaking.

"Lovey, just be more careful next time. These days we have mad cunts about, get out of this fucken town. I was dumped here years ago lovey by my partner, the prick. Never got enough money to leave and now it is too late. I live with an abusive old bloke who owns the pub, treats me like shit, I've even thought of suicide of late. Forget this, men can be real arseholes, don't make my mistake lovey" Margaret told Pauline as she dropped her off at her Winnebago and with a wave was gone.

Pauline at this time now recovering her senses actually felt sorry for Margaret, hard and tough but helplessly trapped in a life of abuse and control.

Pauline stood pondering her situation then decided she needed some help, knocking on Bill's caravan door she entered, "Pauline" Sophie shrieked, "for God's sake what happened to you?"

"I was attacked but don't panic I was saved by Margaret and she brought me home" Pauline replied, telling them the story while Bill was lifting the bed and removing medical equipment. "Okay Sophie, lay towels on the bed please and get me a bowl of warm water quickly" Bill directed.

"Bill, Pauline needs medical attention. For heaven's sake there must be a hospital hereabouts" said Sophie. Wearing only a brief pair of panties and not really knowing what to do, she lost control and sobbed loudly.

"Sophie my dearest friend, Bill is far better trained to clean me up and check my injuries than any in this or any other town and I'd like to keep this amongst ourselves, no real harm done" Pauline soothed her friend.

"How can poor Bill help Pauline, you need medical attention?" a distraught Sophie asked as she laid towels on the bed as instructed.

"Sophie, Bill is a highly specialised Surgeon and very well known in Broome" Pauline replied.

Sophie stood spell bound staring at Bill who looked

confused now as he pulled Sophie to him, "I just thought in my stupid way if you knew perhaps it may have changed your attitude towards me. I was going to tell you Sophie, you see I want you two girls to work in my surgery, running the office if you will when we get home. I intend to work a few days each week and what better staff than you two to do all the book work and make appointments.

"It would have made no difference Bill I loved you from the first night we chatted. Me, your receptionist and working with Pauline!" Sophie exclaimed. "That would be amazing."

"Now let's have our first patient naked on the bed please," Bill taking charge informed Sophie "and very carefully sponge her down".

Pauline lay on the bed as they both ever so gently cleaned her up and couldn't help noticing Bill had the most beautiful long, warm fingers and soft touch. She well understood what Sophie loved about this gentleman.

"Okay Pauline, I want Sophie to hold a light over your vagina so I can see what damage has been done" Bill advised.

He cleaned up around the entrance, his soft fingers pulling her gently apart, and swabbed the area with some antiseptic.

"Okay Pauline clothes on if you want, perhaps a pair of Sophie's panties. You can sleep here tonight my girl, shock may set in later but you are resilient so hopefully not. You have a very small tear but it should heal quickly. No sex for at least three weeks and all will be fine" Bill informed her peeling off his gloves.

"Thanks Bill you are a gem. Sleep may be hard to find tonight, I'm still a bit shaken up but if there is a plus to this it has taught me to be more careful" Pauline replied.

"I have a couple of tablets that will calm you down and help you to sleep but tomorrow you travel with me and Sophie will drive your truck" Bill instructed.

Sophie with Bill's help made up a bed for Pauline and fussing about made her comfortable. The last thing Pauline remembered was seeing Bill sitting in bed reading a paper while Sophie lay on his chest. The scene made Pauline feel safe and comfortable and as the medication kicked in she slumbered off.

Chapter Nine

Pauline woke to the sound of Sophie singing sweetly and the smell of roasted coffee and toast. Sitting up she gave a little moan as she was still sore from her ordeal.

"How is the patient this morning?" Bill chortled.

"Fine, although a bit stiff and sore but feeling much better thanks to you two" Pauline replied as Sophie sat some coffee and toast on the bedside table.

"Pauline in all sincerity I must admit that morally we should report what happened last night but in reality, having given evidence in such matters when taken to trial, the system tends to paint the victim as the guilty party. I have seen women reduced to nervous wrecks by ruthless bloody Solicitors. Personally I feel we should keep this in house and forget it" Bill informed them.

"I agree with what you say Bill. No great damage done and I am a big girl so this will just be a good lesson for me, will not even tell Mum" Pauline replied.

"Okay we agree, now Pauline pants off, I love looking at your vagina. Let's see how we are faring in the fanny department!" Bill laughed, pulling on gloves.

"Just as long as you only look my Billy boy, Sophie's fanny is the only one you are getting into from now on" Sophie countered.

Again Bill gently applied soothing cream to Pauline and she dressed, Sophie having brought her some clothes.

"Just one thing before we leave guys" Pauline informed

them, "I have to go and thank Margaret. I owe her big time."

Both agreed and Bill unhooked his van in order to drive Pauline back to the hotel. It was after 9am when they tapped on the rear door of the hotel.

Margaret came to the door in an old dressing gown that had seen better days.

"Hi lovey, how are you?" she smiled.

"Margaret, how can I ever repay you? I had to come and see you before we left" Pauline told her.

"I knew the prick was leering at you lovey, something told me to go and check when you left" Margaret remarked.

"Look Margaret, I am going to Broome, want to come with me?" Pauline asked, "I have room and it's on me, won't cost you anything."

"Too late lovey can't change now, my life is fucked. Thanks heaps, but I have made my nest and will stay in it. To be honest lovey too scared at my age to change, I get a bed and food so have to count my blessings. God bless you anyway" Margaret replied.

Pauline felt sad for her saviour, "Here is my phone number Margaret, keep it safe. I will send money for your fare if you ever want to leave, I will always owe you!" Pauline responded as both hugged each other.

So far this trip had taught her some tough lessons. A whole world of danger and tragedy existed, something her closeted life had shielded her from. Even Bill and Sophie did not speak much. Bill looked protectively at the two girls who had become part of his life and hooking up the caravan made tracks back to the park.

"Listen girls, what are your thoughts? Like you I was taking my time but now I feel like heading home with my lovely Sophie. What do you think about taking the inland road to Port Headland and straight to Broome?"

"For me spot on, I can't wait to see my new home. What about you Pauline?" Sophie replied enthusiastically.

"My thoughts too, Bill. I miss my Mum but to have a life with you two, let's fucking go! My new career awaits, and maybe some nuddy swimming on Cable Beach!" Pauline exclaimed feeling enthused.

"Bill might not like us girls showing our tits in public" Sophie giggled.

"Bill loves nude swimming, did it all the time with my late wife" Bill chipped in. "I'm proud of your titties Sophie and your bum, for that matter. If you've got it Sophie and you too Pauline, flaunt it" he added.

Bill pulled out and headed north with a new sense of purpose. Pauline dozed in the passenger seat. Even after her trauma she had settled safe in the knowledge that not only would she soon see her mother but a job awaited her working alongside her two best friends.

Pauline slept soundly, the hum of the vehicle dulling her into complete relaxation as the little convoy sped north. Reaching Kalgoorlie she got out, stretching her legs while Sophie and Bill fuelled both vehicles. They hoped to stop off road that evening and make Port Headland turnoff the following evening. Now that the course was set, all three wanted only to reach Broome and start their new life.

Pauline had secretly decided not to return to Canberra. In fact she had sent an SMS to a real estate agent and sold the house, surprisingly within twenty four hours of the listing.

A removalist had been hired to pack, remove and store her furniture and belongings. She would decide later what to do with them but for the time being she now felt completely free financially and with no ties to her old life.

Pauline tried to convince her travelling companions she was fit to drive but both steadfastly refused, so instead she chatted to Bill seeing him in a whole different perspective. This quiet unassuming man who shared with them his weaknesses and strengths had impacted deeply on Pauline. She knew now how lucky indeed Sophie had been in meeting Bill and even understood why she had seen the potential of a relationship with him so quickly. No doubt Pauline decided, because of working her way around Australia alone and of her sexual experiences with men over a protracted period, unlike Pauline who was an innocent until a few months ago.

Pauline even broached the subject of politics with Bill who quietly informed her he believed the arrogance of some politicians was only surpassed by their complete stupidity and incompetence. Liars, spin merchants and rorters. One only had to look at the present party in power, plus the court system choked with members of the same party, all in complete denial of their wrong doing and treating the people who voted them in, like imbeciles.

Pauline decided to avoid the subject with him again but was not surprised in their travels whenever the subject was raised, especially amongst the older set, that his response was always the same.

Pauline, reflecting on her own life, slowly began believing that in fact Bill and thousands of others were absolutely right. Even the bureaucracy she worked in for over two decades had slipped into a huge machine of duck-shoving, public service speak and jargon unable to deliver the most basic of services without cost blowouts and rorting. Completely dysfunctional, full of self-importance and outraged with anyone who pointed out the truth.

By the time evening started to creep over the land Pauline felt tired, even though she had rested all day, and was glad when the convoy came to a halt.

Sophie parked next to the caravan and jumping out gave Bill a big sloppy kiss, both so infatuated with each other that the age difference paled into insignificance. They brought new feelings and companionship into each other's lives just as, Pauline knew, David and Jane had brought into theirs. She dared not hope she may be so lucky but instead delighted in the two most important women in her life finding such wonderful soul mates.

Pauline excused herself and retired to her Winnebago. After having a glass of water she slipped between the sheets and was asleep in five minutes. She woke early, refreshed and keen to continue the journey. She felt ready now to start a new life. So far the trip had been eventful, good times and bad but somehow her instincts told her it was time to meet up with her anxious mother waiting for her in Broome.

Slipping into her shorts and shirt Pauline pulled on her new Rossi boots and with coffee in hand opened Bill's caravan door but quickly retreated and quietly closed it when she saw Sophie sitting on Bill's naked form, rocking backwards and forwards, oblivious of her presence.

Pauline returned to her Winnebago and made some tea and toast then having finished her breakfast she washed up and packed away. Keen to get going, she tapped loudly on the caravan door but was surprised when Sophie gasped, "Not yet, won't be a tick!" Pauline smiled. 'These older men certainly have staying power' she thought!

Deciding to travel on slowly and let Bill and Sophie catch up, Pauline started the motor home. Pulling out she gave a toot on the horn and hit the highway, already busy with mining vehicles and trucks.

Pauline travelled slowly as the sun heated up. She was enjoying the open spaces and landscape. In a reflective mood she thought about the sudden changes to her life and liked the challenge of the unknown. It stimulated her making her appreciate that life was to be enjoyed even though bad things sometimes happen. Half her life was behind her now and like Sophie and her mother she must grasp every opportunity to be happy. Happiness she knew can be fleeting and she must seize it if and when it came.

Approaching a large river Pauline spied tall trees and shade so decided to pull off and stretch her legs. Surprisingly Bill and Sophie pulled in behind her. "Hope I didn't alarm you but it was a lovely morning so I decided to come on ahead" she informed them.

"Actually I told Bill that but he panicked anyway so we came straight on. Not to worry we can have a coffee and our breakfast here, it's such a nice spot" Sophie replied.

"Sorry guys. Must confess I did poke my head in the

caravan to let you know but you were both busy!" Pauline laughed at a blushing Bill.

"Yep got us Pauline, when my girl pleasures me I get so involved that time seems of no consequence" Bill explained.

"No worries Bill, honestly if I were in her position we would still be back there" Pauline laughed.

The three friends chatted away all anxious to end the journey for different reasons. Pauline again pulled onto the highway and assured them both she was fine. Even her pussy was feeling better she added, causing a ripple of laughter amongst the trio.

It was about 3pm before Pauline pulled over again, this time backing under a huge tree beside a river. It was a truly peaceful spot.

"Pauline I reckon we are only about thirty kilometres from the Great Northern Highway. Although it is only early, quiet spots to camp from here on will be scarce and crowded so just as a suggestion, perhaps we should consider staying here and heading off early in the morning. Port Headland is one big traffic jam with mining trucks, roadworks and the rest going on. Better to pass straight through" Bill suggested.

"I'm with you guys" Pauline replied, "to be honest, I'm just beginning to feel tired."

"I'll prepare dinner after we have a walk by the river" Sophie offered.

"You two go. I'll stay here and guard the fleet" Bill laughed, "this area will fill up in the next hour."

Pauline and Sophie walked off holding hands enjoying

girls' time alone as they walked down the river, finally sitting under a tree in the cool shade.

"Since I met you Sophie my life has really changed. I am so glad you and Bill still want me in your lives. Boring old me! Pauline added.

"Pauline you are and always will be my best friend, in fact I class you as my sister. Nothing will ever part us I promise" Sophie insisted hugging Pauline tightly.

"What a find in Bill, really if we had not shagged those blokes we may never have met him" Pauline giggled.

"Yep, that was over the hill exciting shagging but what I have now is far more intimate and loving. Bill really satisfies me, he leaves me with an afterglow that is hard to explain and somehow Pauline I give my whole body to him. To be honest I've had a few men in my life but never experienced the loving and pure pleasure we share" Sophie confided.

"I understand really I do. Our shagathon at Streaky Bay was wild sex but only sex. I long for what you have Sophie, and Mum as far as that goes, we all need a special person in our lives. We do all need sex but not at any cost" Pauline replied.

Sophie smiled, "I agree and intend to pamper my man and give him the best time in bed. I watch Bill as I get undressed. We both sleep in the nude and when we touch it is electric. I become wet, watching him gazing at me as I move towards him. Honest Pauline, I am dripping by the time he enters me."

"I am so happy for you Sophie, any chance of a baby?" Pauline asked.

"Bill told me if I want one he would be happy but to think about him not being around as he or she grows up. I know he would love a child as he has no family left so 'yes', I am off the pill, let's see what happens. Possibly to some this may be rushing things but time is a wonderful thing if you have plenty of it. Like you Pauline, my eggs are numbered and time is critical" Sophie told her.

"Never gave it much thought, I suppose because I never had someone to fertilise me but I would love to hold my own baby Sophie. I have little time left for that, who knows what might happen, but being an aunty will do for the time being" Pauline smiled in deep reflection at the news, secretly now aware she may never know motherhood.

Returning to the caravan and motor home both sat down under the awning Bill had erected, sipping drinks he too had prepared.

Bill outlined his plans for a clinic. He wanted to set up a private practice as a GP and perhaps spend one day a week as a Visiting Surgeon at the local hospital doing minor surgery.

"Treating more vaginas, Bill?" Pauline asked.

"No naughty Pauline" Bill chuckled, adding "although I suppose nice ones like yours would be okay and of course, Sophie's."

Lights twinkled as the grey nomad army was on the move. The three friends waved at each new caravan pulling in. By sunset the place was crowded.

As daylight streaked over the valleys, Pauline and Bill pulled out and by 7am hit the main highway, snaking north towards their final destination.

Reaching Port Headland they fuelled up before proceeding and with trucks and machinery everywhere they both sighed with relief when they again hit the highway. They planned to spend the final night of the trip at the Sandfire Roadhouse and so decided to keep driving as far as possible before lunch.

Chapter Ten

They stopped for lunch at a pull off but with no shade the sun beat down mercilessly. The three anxious to get on the road again as soon as possible decided only to have a cold drink and snack. They drank and ate in silence. The quest now was to get the trip over with. Their mindset had changed and, now anxious to reach Broome, they drove on.

It was late in the afternoon when they reached Sandfire and having looked at the area, a quick conversation ensued and a decision made that if Sophie were to share the driving, they would travel on. Pauline chatted to Bill whilst Sophie drove her rig and so they drank coffee and changed drivers frequently. At last they arrived at the Roebuck Roadhouse having again changed drivers, and drinking strong coffee they were all on a high, with Broome only thirty kilometres away.

At 1am a tired crew arrived at Cable Beach. Bill pulled into his drive and Pauline locked her van out on the street. Sophie gave a shout and rushed to Bill as he unlocked and turned on the power. Pauline looked in amazement, the house was beautiful. Even a pool undercover shimmered in the light.

Pauline, mentally and physically tired, in the heat of the moment stripped off and jumped into the pool, the cool water taking her breath away. Looking around, as Bill and Sophie naked followed with a splash of water, Pauline swam to the other end, reinvigorated and deliriously happy. As she looked up her Mum and David were standing there with a tray of bottles and glasses. Placing the tray on a bench they too tore their clothes off and plunged in. Mayhem followed with them all splashing each other, Pauline hugging her mother and David, even though all were naked and laughing like madmen.

Bill was standing at the end of the pool, tears streaming down his face, deliriously happy at the scene before him. Jane swam up the pool and hugging a surprised Bill dragged him back into the action. He and David shook each other by the hand.

"Bill, never thought we would meet again under these circumstances or in this way" David laughed.

"David old friend, what bloody wonderful women we have found. Un-bloody real, can't come to terms with my luck" Bill beamed.

"Yep, bloody mad lot of ravers Bill. Just here in time, we are getting married next week." David announced jumping out and placing the wine and glasses at the side of the pool.

"Mum that was the 'news'!!" Pauline shrieked as both girls again hugged and kissed Jane.

David filled the glasses and all stood naked in the pool toasting everything from the wedding to all meeting, to the weather, laughing and shouting in glee. Pauline felt she was home at last chuckling to herself as she looked at David's hanging penis, thinking all I need is one like that. One by one they got out of the pool picking up scattered clothing and all talking at once. Jane disappeared and returned with more bottles of wine and plates of food.

"I made up the beds with fresh sheets and turned the hot water on Bill, we also put some food in the fridge and vacuumed out, well not really," Jane admitted "got a cleaner in to do most of it." No one even thought of sleep. All the news was swapped except Pauline's sexual activities and her assault. Even so, hilarious laughter erupted at some of their exploits.

"Now how did you two start a relationship Bill?" David asked inquisitively, "and the truth please!" "Well David to be honest, it was me" Sophie chipped in half tanked. "When I first saw Bill I decided to go for him and he had no chance, shagged him the second night!"

Everyone collapsed in laughter. One thing for sure Bill decided, Sophie was honest, perhaps too honest. What a woman! In fact, he corrected as he looked around the room, three great women. 'No wonder David went for Jane' he mused, 'something about her and her movement made her erotic and sexy like Pauline, lucky bugger too who beds her!'

Five o'clock came and shards of sunlight pierced through the curtains but still no one made a move to go to bed. All relaxed sitting by the pool talking, enjoying each other's company and discussing the coming wedding. Jane informed Pauline she was to be her attendant and Ross, David's son would attend him. Just then a middle aged man appeared at the sliding door wearing shorts, a western shirt and sunglasses atop his Akubra. Pauline stared, he was an absolute hunk. "Off now Dad, see you all at the wedding" he called from the door.

101

"Oh come over here mate for a sec, meet our two new arrivals Pauline and Sophie. You can welcome Bill home too" David quipped.

Ross Anderson came forward awkwardly, putting out his hand. Pauline gulped for air now embarrassed that she had a thong on and a skimpy top, her confidence for once shot completely. No one warned me about this man, for fuck's sake, 'he has to have a wife and kids', she thought!

"Hi Pauline and Sophie" Ross shook each by the hand, "glad to see you home Bill, will have to catch up at the wedding, big day coming up with a muster on".

With that he turned around and walked towards the door, Pauline staring after him. 'He was perfect' she thought, 'but sadly out of reach or Mum would have told me about him'. All the others returned to their chatting but Pauline watched him go. As he reached the door he looked back and embarrassed he had been caught, walked right into it. Only Pauline had witnessed the event and as he straightened up she smiled at him and her heart beat a dozen times faster when he smiled back. It was only then she imagined what a sight she must have been, in fact all of them, standing around half naked.

At six o'clock Jane suggested bed for a few hours' sleep and that the girls go into the Boulevard later in the day to buy dresses for the wedding. All agreed now as exhaustion overcame them though Pauline was still on a high, her heart racing and her mouth dry. For the first time in her life she was in lust. In lust for Ross, even if he was taken she would find it hard to forget him.

Jane insisted Pauline come over to them in David's

house and she being so tired decided to go along, a few hours' sleep would not hurt. With Pauline still only in her thong and top, David asked her for the keys to the Winnebago so he could park it in his drive until she unpacked it and then so it was safe he insisted it be parked on his big front lawn.

Entering the beautiful home Pauline could see why her Mum was so happy. It was immaculate with modern furniture, not like the Canberra house. On the way in and unable to control herself Pauline whispered to Jane, "What's the deal with Ross. Is there a wife or girlfriend?"

"Ah Pauline, Ross is a hermit and single. Lives on the station alone, only came into town to service his helicopter yesterday and stayed here overnight. He had a couple of girlfriends early but they were young. If you land him 'well done' but don't build up your hopes, I have heard he is hung like a horse and it is rumoured that nothing is taboo with him!" Jane warned her daughter.

"Seriously Mum, I think he is just shy and perhaps like me once, not so long ago, has no idea how to chat to the opposite sex, he seemed so awkward. Look out Ross baby, Pauline is heading your way!" Pauline chuckled.

David came in and the conversation stopped. Pauline jumped into her bed, having passed the room Ross used on his few visits into town. Laying in bed she felt tired but now the adrenalin was pumping. Her Ross was available and about her own age she guessed. Now just as Sophie and her Mum had done with Bill and David, Pauline set her goals to bed Ross. 'Maybe have his children', she mused.

103

Sleep evaded her for some time and even when she did sleep she dreamed of her and Ross making love and woke several times in a sweat, the dreams so real. She cautioned herself that her obsession might not become a reality and to face the fact that it may not happen even with her best endeavours. At one stage she woke in a panic, her heart racing, she had dreamt it had taken her so long to win Ross she had stopped having periods with no chance of any offspring. Getting out of bed she showered and wrapped herself in a towel. Having found her keys on the table, she unlocked her motor home and got dressed ready for the day. Pauline still felt exhausted although excited and with her mind racing, trying to work out a way to get her Ross, she made some coffee then sat thinking and planning. One thing she reasoned, don't rush in and frighten him off. That would be fatal. Yet, a chill ran up her spine, to delay may also be fatal.

It had taken Sophie one day to bed Bill and Jane, her own mother, four hours to bed David, she remembered.

Sophie tapped on the door, "Ready to go yet? Bill has a few jobs to do and will meet me later in the day" Sophie chirped, beaming with happiness.

"What did you think of Ross?" Pauline asked.

"Ross, God 'yes' what a hunk but is he single, surely not?" Sophie responded.

"Yes, single. Sophie I am in love, you have to help me bed him. I've never lusted after a man like this before, what a hunk" Pauline pleaded.

"Oh Pauline what a dream, we could all live together, a real fairytale" Sophie replied. "Well Sophie, this girl is going to do all in her power to catch him" Pauline vowed as her mother entered the kitchen.

"Find everything girls? We will leave shortly after I shower and dress, David has a few things to pick up in town. We are going to the station in the morning to help with the mustering" Jane told them.

"Mum I would love to come too if possible. Sophie and Bill are going to rent a building or office in town for a clinic and before I start work I'd love to see a station" Pauline, nearly begging, replied.

"Of course dear if you want, David will not mind and you can pursue Ross, I know what you are up to. Actually I know the food he loves so let's stock up and you can win his heart in the kitchen. Slowly my girl slowly, this fish I would say is a virgin. Never taken the bait yet, so a little tender teasing may help" Jane chuckled.

Pauline was ecstatic, her smile was radiant, her lust rising, wild encounters soared like eagles in her erotic thoughts, failure was not an option.

While shopping for dresses for the wedding Pauline came out of a shop looking like her mother, in moleskins and a western shirt wearing an Akubra with sunglasses atop along with new boots. Even Jane and Sophie whistled, she looked smashing and, now small and petite with big firm breasts, stares came from everywhere. Pauline 'number three' had arrived!

Two trips to Jane's car were required to carry all the purchases. Pauline had three new western shirts, four pairs of jeans as well as the moleskins she wore, two Akubras, one for best and one for every day plus a pair of designer sunglasses on and a pair as a spare.

Pauline had already booked a visit to a hairstylist and later that afternoon while Sophie and Bill grocery shopped, Jane waited patiently for Pauline who swept out of the salon looking like a model. Arriving home, even David whistled.

"My God Pauline you look ravishing, but quite understandable considering the Mum who produced you" he joked.

Jane on Pauline's instructions purchased heaps of Ross's favourites and placed them in the back of the station ute ready for the early morning start. She said that she and David would take their Landcruiser and asked if Pauline would mind following them and driving the heavily laden ute. Pauline gleefully agreed. 'To be seen to be useful was a good start and, no matter what, she was determined to impress in the cattle yards or wherever', she thought happily.

That evening they joined Bill and a radiant Sophie for dinner by the pool. Bill had one request of Pauline and it was that she at least work for a few weeks to help set up a filing system for the new practice. Sophie had spoken highly of her organisational skills and he said the red tape in setting up a general practice was mind boggling. Bill told those present that he and Sophie were checking out an empty shop in Chinatown to see if it was suitable. Sophie, he said beaming, would furnish and decorate it. 'God help us!' thought Pauline and Jane.

Pauline was so excited she rose at 4am preparing for the day ahead. New jeans, shirt and boots completed her transformation from public servant to outback cattle ringer. David and her mother suggested tactfully that it may be overkill for the cattle yards but Pauline was out to impress Ross and knew exactly what she was doing.

The two vehicles pulled out of the drive at daybreak, David and Jane leading the way, with Pauline following, her heart racing, ready to tackle any problem no matter how insurmountable.

Pauline was shocked at the distance. She seemed to be driving forever and even when they stopped at Fitzroy Crossing was told they still had two hundred kilometres to drive to the station. This was her first contact with full blood Aboriginals, wandering about everywhere. All seemed friendly and some spoke to David and Jane so obviously knew them.

Two hours later in midafternoon they turned off the highway and Pauline dropped back, the dust was making the road invisible. The vast landscape was awesome, huge cliff faces and long mountain ranges covered in red sand making the scene majestic, nothing like she had ever seen before. Her concentration was shattered when two small helicopters came out of the blue thudding overhead causing her to nearly run off the track. They swept south out over the ranges, the hair stood up on her neck as she watched them weave up over the escarpment ahead. This was as foreign to her as visiting another planet. Her excitement grew as they wound their way up over a huge jump up that had been cemented for some reason before she sucked in her breath. Below stood a row of buildings with what looked like a homestead on the banks of a gigantic river

107

like an oasis in the desert and to her left she noticed huge yards full of cattle stirring up a constant cloud of dust.

Pulling in next to David and her mother, she stepped from the vehicle gazing around at the green lawn on which two helicopters were parked side by side.

Looking resplendent, Pauline strode confidently after Jane who steered Pauline to a small room facing the veranda, placing her bags on the bed Jane then guided her around the homestead, first to the huge kitchen and dining room with seating for over thirty people. Pauline gasped at the kitchen pantry shelves stocked like a local supermarket. This Jane informed her was where they would stack the supplies she had carried from Broome.

A long hall had several other bedrooms either side, one being David and hers when they visited. The other larger room belonged to Ross. Jane shook her head as she held the door open, clothes and an unmade bed made it look like a cyclone had gone through the place. Pauline looked at the huge four poster bed with its faded and worn curtains hanging loose and hardly noticed the rest of the tour, she was already imagining making new curtains and cleaning up the room she planned to share with Ross!

After coffee they unloaded the supplies finishing just before dusk. Pauline heard the thump of the big diesel generator and asking her mother what that was for was surprised to learn "It's for the power supply, there's no grid service out here". Pauline felt a bit stupid for asking the question and decided not to ask any more in company in case she made herself look too silly but to note what she needed to know and find out on the quiet. If Ross thought she was stupid perhaps he may lose interest even though as yet she had only solicited a bashful grin. Pauline was bitterly disappointed when she finally returned from the shower at 9pm and Jane informed her Ross had gone to bed. They wanted to start drafting at daylight so he had a quick bite, showered in her room and retired.

Five other single rooms ran along the veranda from her bedroom and while undressing she heard several doors slam as other people crashed after a long day.

Pauline lay for some time before finally drifting off to sleep. She was rudely awoken by banging on her door and it took her a few seconds to remember where she was after the previous day's happenings. Pulling on her clothes and brushing her hair, she washed in the sink before applying some makeup. Certain principles must be adhered to she told herself, even here in the wilderness.

As she entered the kitchen Ross, two Aboriginal ringers and two backpackers plus, she was to learn, a chopper pilot were filing out, all nodding to her as they jumped in various vehicles and headed to the yards. Pauline's heart skipped a beat fearing competition when she saw a young Swedish backpacker with the shortest pair of shorts and a swimming bikini top on, busily washing up. Turning she saw Pauline and said, "I'm Ingrid, you want breakfast yah?"

Pauline nodded as a plate of bacon and eggs hit the table along with a mug of black coffee. It was then her mother arrived.

"Oh you've met Ingrid the cook, dear. Better hurry, the boys are counting on you. They are a bit short, two backpackers left yesterday. David went long ago to set up, I will bring morning tea down later" Jane said stirring milk and sugar into her cup of coffee.

'Fuck this! Game on! Ingrid is dripping bloody sex into the trenches. This is total bloody war, better get to the yards and show Ross my worth' Pauline thought and grabbing a piece of bacon ran outside, no fucking transport she frowned!

Jogging, she headed towards the distant cloud of dust and thundering cattle. Approaching the perimeter fence she noticed one of the Aboriginal stockmen running her way through the milling, bellowing mob.

"Hold up missus, get bloody killed in this mob, eh" he yelled.

"What do you mean?" Pauline shouted above the dust and mayhem.

"You get um fucken trampled by big fella bull" the stockman roared back.

Well how the fuck do I get in and what is your name?" Pauline hollowed back frustrated.

"Me name Sonny, you come along me, missus boss" he directed.

Pauline did not know it at the time but this was the start of a friendship that would last for decades.

Indicating to follow him along the fence and watch the mob for big fella scrub bulls or even mad cows, Sonny led the way. Pauline now not so confident watched the milling mob, some wild-eyed snorted at them and all of a sudden one broke from the mob charging at them. Sonny indicated to Pauline to get up on the fence and she needed no reminding as she grabbed the top rail and launched herself up as the mad beast hit the rail below. Unfortunately Pauline kept going over in the momentum and landed head first in the dust and cow shit. Her new hat covered in crap and her sunglasses broken, she remembered Sonny picking her up. With her new clothes absolutely rat-shit, she looked like a derelict. Even her lovely blonde hair dark red now with bits of cow shit knotted in the once stylish hairdo.

Dusting herself off she was shaking as Sonny again indicated to get up on the fence. Pauline found a new sense of power as she saw a crazed heifer coming at them, ears bleeding, as it was let go from the crush. Pauline this time held on gamely to the top rail and looking around saw several of the workers grinning. Ross had his head down tagging and David's back was to them as he operated a crush holding each yearling in as they came through. Pauline was unsure but thought Ross 'had a stupid grin on his face'. That was it for Pauline "I'll show this lot of pricks" she fumed, dusting herself off and following Sonny. Gritting her teeth she called "Laugh, will you? Arseholes".

Sonny took her down to the rear end of the long race aware Pauline was absolutely green to this whole procedure.

"Me and Billy, we silly buggers. Bring um up from big yard into forcing yard alonga here missus, you pull gate here, let five go in eh, then push gate shut, this stop em piling up and hurting each other, then push em up to that fella up on drafting race. He put old breeder cow one way, yearlings go to big boss who earmark and tag,

111

old cows go alonga back to run with old bulls, yearlings they come back through, sort heifer from bull fella, then preg-test heifer, no take boat with calf inside hey."

"Thanks Sonny, what is a bull, a heifer and an old cow?" Pauline asked.

Sonny shook his head, "Bull fella has balls see", he pointed "and dick hanga under. Heifer, she have fanny under tail."

Just at that time a big bull mounted a heifer in the forcing yards. Pauline looked wide-eyed as he mounted and drove his big long dick into the heifer causing her to hunch her back and hold her tail up.

"Fella on top him bull, heifer been fucked under." Sonny pointed out, quite serious.

Sonny and Billy pushed them up as Pauline counted five and slammed the gate shut. Sonny gave the thumbs up and Pauline regained a bit of confidence. I'll show this lot she promised herself, choking in the dust, her clothes wrecked and smelling like a dead cow.

The routine went on for several hours and Pauline was choking for water but too proud to ask anyone. She had her part to play and only death would prevent her from carrying it out.

David yelled "Smoko" mid-morning as Jane pulled up with lunch. Pauline was starving and weak from thirst as Sonny and Billy jumped the fence and indicated for her to follow them.

"God Pauline, what happened to you?" Jane asked in alarm.

"Nothing Mum thank you, just fell over, no big problem"

she bravely rasped grabbing a bottle of water and gulping it down.

"Always take water to drink out here Pauline, you need quite a few litres daily." Jane told her passing a large water container.

Pauline was fuming. Ross had hardly acknowledged her. He was too busy talking to his father and seemed anxious to get back to work. She overheard a truck was booked for the following afternoon to take twelve decks. She reminded herself to find out what a bloody deck was for later when she started a conversation with him. 'Steady' she thought, 'listen to Mum, slow and easy. This bugger is no easy, in the sack and bingo, quick fuck!'

Turning her back, Pauline tore into some meat sandwiches which stopped her hunger craving. Seeing Sonny and Billy heading back she followed trying to show all present that Pauline was a good worker and helper. On the way she sidled up to Sonny who now took it upon himself to try and educate Pauline, he liked her toughness. In his culture women had to be tough.

"What is a deck?" she enquired.

"Deck of plurry cards, or may be cattle. Cattle they be one deck in a road train, maybe three trailers, so three top decks, three bottoms" Sonny proudly informed her.

"How many maybe decks?" Pauline asked trying to learn as much as possible.

"These little weaners or yearling weigh about two fifty to three fifty kilos and about three hundred for one semi, say six decks" Sonny responded, proudly imparting his knowledge.

Once again they started the routine amongst the dust and the noise, reaching a crescendo. Pauline soon began to realise how skilled Sonny and Billy were pushing up the range cattle. Some perhaps, she was to learn, in human contact for the first time in their lives as well as being stirred up by helicopters barking overhead pushing them into the holding yards. These cattle she learnt had been left for two days to quieten down before drafting to avoid damaging them.

Whenever they had to wait till those further up the line caught up Pauline chatted to Sonny. Billy was quiet and shy but Sonny forthcoming. She even knew he was showing off his skills sometimes by throwing dirt in a bull's face causing him to charge so he could sidestep the charging animal. She often laughed as his skinny little legs flew up the yard railing.

The sun was setting over the escarpment as the last lot passed Pauline. She was exhausted, she'd been sweating all day, she felt disgusting, was covered in dust and her clothes smelled so bad she felt sick.

"Go home Pauline, finish now we come along soon" Sonny told her.

Pauline took no convincing. She walked across the now empty holding yard to the fence and scaling it, she dropped to the other side. Finding the keys in Ross's vehicle she jumped in and smiling, drove back to the homestead.

Pauline went to her room showered and collapsed on the bed. When her mother came in later with some food she was snoring, fast asleep, laying spread-eagled on the bed. Placing the tray of food on the table she silently closed the door.

Jane felt sorry for Pauline but a little of her late father's know-all attitude existed in her daughter and rather felt perhaps the lesson had to be learned the hard way.

Pauline woke early to movement next door and glancing at her watch saw it was 5.30am. Struggling to get out of bed, she dressed this time in shorts and shirt, pulling on her boots still covered in shit and dust. She crammed the filthy hat on and added a new pair of sunnies. Eating the meal left on her table last night she quietly filled her canteen and was in the yards waiting, smirking as the others arrived.

Chapter Eleven

Standing defiantly as Ross entered the yards, Pauline drew herself up, hands on hips, looking straight at him, "What do you want me to do today?" she asked.

Ross gulped, "Ah perhaps stand by the drafting race and tell Colin what is coming, male or female. The rest can keep them running and Dad and I will help the Vet preg-test the heifers" Ross replied.

"Yeh, stand here Pauline and as they approach the drafting race, just yell out the sex" Colin instructed as he climbed up to his chair.

The others got into position. The bulls would go right Sonny informed her and the heifers onto the crush to be tested. Loading would commence after lunch, so they had to keep moving.

Pauline placed herself in position as the first animal came belting down the race,

"Balls," she shouted, as Colin nearly fell off the seat. "Fanny" she yelled, staring straight ahead as the line slowly trotted past. If she had looked up she'd have noticed that all in ear shot were doubled over laughing as Pauline, half bending, concentrated one hundred percent on her job.

For three hours Pauline yelled "Balls" or "Fanny" until the line had passed.

Straightening up she swayed from left to right limbering up her tired muscles after so much concentration, then she looked down the line at the crush. A man who she gathered was the vet was shoving his arm up a cow's arse then withdrawing it covered in shit while the horrified animal was released into pens either side. Then just as quickly, after some lube occasionally, up the bum again. Pauline stood transfixed, mouth open, not knowing what to do or think. If this was pregnancy testing, she shuddered, no fucking kids for old Pauline!

Pauline strode past the three men testing the heifers. 'Sick bastards' she thought, 'fuck me, what next?' Her mother arrived with lunch followed by a convoy of huge rigs ready to start loading. As she moved past, Ross turned to Sonny, "You and Billy, Colin and Pauline start loading after lunch," he yelled above the noise of the trucks lining up ready to load "load the bulls first, we will keep going and should finish in an hour." Sonny nodded and they jumped the fence to enjoy a cuppa and some fresh sandwiches.

Pauline was still numb, contemplating the scene she had just witnessed. Not just a little way in but up to the elbow, she shuddered again at the thought. Still this muster business only lasts two months a year so toughen up girl! 'Fuck' she thought 'when I get back to town I'm on the bloody pill again, fuck this hand up the arse routine.'

Pauline however did notice the pregnant heifers were let go and she watched them running down the laneway to join the breeding cows and bulls. Perhaps pregnancy in relation to the heifers saved them from the chop. An arm up the rectum and pregnancy as far as cows go may not be so bad after all.

Pauline was given the job of standing at the bottom of

the loading ramp. With instructions from Sonny, who now felt it his solemn duty to teach Pauline the art of working in cattle yards, to slide the gate across should a bottleneck happen or if any cattle tried to turn around or back down the race.

The truckie of the first truck passed Pauline a cattle prod telling her to give any hesitant animal a 'touch on the arse', as he politely put it. Holding the stick she gave one a poke with no results. "Turn it on" the truckie yelled through the bellowing and dust. Pauline looked at the handle and seeing the on-off switch, pushed it forward. "Now try it" the truckie suggested.

Pauline touched the two protruding barbs on the end of the prodder and nearly turned completely over backwards with the shock. "I meant on the bloody cattle" the truckie quipped.

Undaunted, Pauline regained her composure ready for her task, unwilling to admit defeat. Yet she knew, if any of the things that had happened to her since she had been here had happened in Canberra it would have forced an inquiry at a cost tens of thousands of dollars for reports and work place safety investigations, as well as on months of stress leave and perhaps because of so much trauma, some may never have worked again.

Actually when she got into the routine she enjoyed the banter with the truckies. As each one loaded, filled in the paper work and Ross, she noticed signed it, a new truck was ready to pull in and the loading would again commence.

The pressure was on but Pauline was busting for a pee.

She had noticed the men just stood with their backs to her and peed, so gaining confidence she rushed around the opposite side of the truck during a lull in loading whilst the truckie forced cattle forward and closed gates.

Squatting under the truck she pulled her shorts and panties down feeling a rush of relief as her gush hit the ground. At the same time however a torrent of cattle piss hit her still squirting pee. She jumped clear but was soaked.

Pulling up her panties and shorts she knew she had two choices. Go home and change or go back to work and hope that no one thankfully had seen the event. The piss she assumed would dry quickly in the sun, even though it smelt shocking.

Pauline chose the second. To admit defeat now was unthinkable. What would the man who was to marry her think! What a stupid thing not to think there were cattle above and inevitably cattle pee and poop. 'You idiot Pauline' she fumed.

Returning to her post, trying to look dignified, she in fact appeared like a drowned rat. Urine had mixed with the cattle shit and now covered her Akubra with a dark brown stain and had splattered her shirt.

The truckie looked down at her and unable to control himself, laughed loudly. "Next time stay out from under the truck mate" he yelled for all to hear. Pauline stood defiantly and shouted, "Are you here to be a smart arse or load fucking cattle? Just get on with it." A grin hit his face when he heard Pauline. 'Small but feisty' he thought, 'I like this little big-titted sheila'. "Calm down ducky, meant no harm, tough little bugger, admit that" he yelled back.

Three hours later and again so tired she had a headache, Pauline was grateful to see the last of the trucks slowly snake its way down the road heading for the yards in Broome. Somehow she felt sad for the yearlings on board, only days ago they ran fancy free in the wild. However, becoming more of a realist every day, she knew any country in reality must produce and sell something to pay the salaries of people like herself, who in all her working life produced nothing but paperwork.

David drove up to her, "Jump in mate got to take my hat off to you, you have certainly proved you can match it with the rest of us" he told her.

"In a strange way I enjoyed it actually, might look like shit but I feel good I have done it and that I didn't give up" Pauline smiled through the muck and dust.

Returning to her room Pauline stood under the shower feeling rejuvenated. David had made her feel better, his little bit of praise proving she could match it with the rest of them gave her a good feeling, even though she had to admit that only her stubborn pride and trying to please Ross had made her keep going.

Ingrid and Jane had dinner on the table as she entered. Ravenous she tucked into a large steak, disappointed to learn Ross was in the office paying off the staff. Jane informed her only one muster remained to be done on an isolated section of the property but Ross worked for a muster company and they had called him up to help with a muster near Broome, so he was leaving at day break.

Pauline bade a farewell to Sonny and Billy. She gave them both a big hug and thanked them for all their help and perhaps even saving her life.

Ingrid was catching a ride into Broome with Jane and David but Colin was going to stay for a few days to caretake the station in Ross's absence.

Pauline was happy to see Ingrid who she viewed as a competitor for Ross's affections heading to Broome. Colin came out from the office and said to Pauline, "Ross wants you in the office if you have time".

Pauline's heart raced, 'He has seen the light' she thought, wants to see me alone!

Ross had his head down and as she walked in his smile made her heart skip a beat. "I paid you like the rest, I know it is not much for the long hours but $200 a day is usual" he said passing her a cheque.

Pauline was gob smacked. Without even sitting down she fumed as she tore up the cheque and threw it at him, "I did not come out here to get paid thank you Ross. I have been fucken trampled, electrocuted, pissed on and fuck knows what else you ungrateful prick. Not even a thank you and I really liked you too." she wailed.

Never confronted like this before Ross shuffled uncomfortably behind the desk. Since he had first seen Pauline he felt attracted to her but still a virgin and woefully shy and uneducated with women he was unsure how to handle this situation.

"And finally I was going to cook you your favourite foods, even brought some with me but you had sexy Ingrid, fuck you and this place".

Pauline regained control and left the office going straight to her bedroom. Closing the door she collapsed on the bed, shattered. At least he could have said thanks instead offering her fucking money.

Pauline heard a tap on the door it, was her mother, "Don't blame Ross he is just not used to dealing with women. The ones that come here are backpackers and he pays them all, that's why they come. Pauline, you have to understand Ross. His life is just work, nothing else. He is kind-hearted believe me but this is his life and his sole focus."

"Sorry Mum silly old me, had great illusions for once in my life. Oh well at least I have a job in Broome and still on pay for a month from Canberra" Pauline accepting her situation replied. They hugged each other before her mother left the room.

It was a long night for Pauline, her head ached and she was confused wondering if there was something wrong with her, why men did not find her attractive other than for sex.

Showering on daylight she dressed and packed her bags. A tap came on the door, it was Jane, "Ross sent me to ask you if you want a helicopter ride back to Broome, I reckon it might be his way of saying sorry" Jane told her.

Pauline was about to tell her Mum to tell him to fuck off but relented. It was a long drive back to Broome and an aerial view would be exciting. The ride would let her see country she had never seen before.

"Okay Mum, when is he leaving?" Pauline replied.

"He is doing his final check now, hurry you will just

have time for a coffee and toast. I will take your bags in the cruiser back to Broome" Jane replied.

Pauline raced to the kitchen and although she was not feeling hungry she managed to drink half a cup of coffee before she heard the chopper start. Hurrying to the plane Ross beckoned her to the passenger side. With the rotors whirling overhead and closing the door, he leant over her fastening her seat belt, then placed headphones gently over her head. She heard him ask, "Okay, can you hear me?"

"Yes thank you" Pauline replied. She was going to apologise for the previous evening but decided to wait to see what happened, perhaps he would say sorry first.

As the motor roared into life and they rose straight into the air Pauline gasped in surprise, forgetting everything as a new vista opened before her and streaking along was mesmerised at the beauty of the place. Something stirred within her, a feeling of contentment as they skimmed above the massive landscape below, awe inspiring almost biblical in its element. Pauline was transfixed, taking in the vista as it changed crossing the mountain ranges.

"That is the run we are mustering next, you can see the outstation below" said Ross waking her from the dream like state she was in.

Dropping fast he circled the yards and huts below before heading west towards Broome.

"I will take you over the Ord Dam on the way and the Bungle Bungles" Ross told her.

Pauline was really unsure what he was talking about but thought it best to question him on what she envisaged he felt happy to talk about.

123

"How big is the station?" Pauline questioned.

Jane was right this was Ross's life. He talked animatedly for many minutes explaining acres, cattle numbers, various runs and their attributes and problems, all foreign to Pauline but she began to appreciate that Ross was a different man to any she had ever met and knew she was falling in love.

"How often do you contract out?" she asked after a small break to take in all the info she had gleaned.

"Only if they are short, have plenty of my own to keep me going but the cash is handy. Prices have been a bit low for some time" Ross informed her.

They then chatted about cattle prices, costs and a myriad of other things as Ross pointed to the Ord Dam below and soon after to the Argyle Diamond Mine and then the Bungle Bungles.

Although the trip was at the reaches of the fuel supply the Robison carried, all too soon Pauline saw the cattle station at Roebuck Bay and other helicopters parked outside the hangar.

As the rotors slowly came to a halt Pauline was surprised when Ross alighted and ran around to her side helping her from the little machine.

"The mechanic will run you home" Ross told her as she walked to the hangar.

The mechanic approached, "Grant said to go down to Eighty Mile Beach, he'll catch you up down there" he told Ross.

"Okay after I fuel up I'll head" Ross replied.

"Come on Pauline let's get you home" the mechanic said as he ushered her to the car.

Pauline was disappointed when Ross waved her goodbye and stood watching as he strode back to the helicopter, stopping to roll a drum of avgas towards the machine as he went. 'It may take her a little time to work him out' she thought as they drove into Broome.

Arriving home to an empty house Pauline decided to take a nap before contacting Sophie and Bill. She knew it would be later in the afternoon before her mother and David arrived. She knew also that she would see Ross again the following week at the wedding but that now seemed like an eternity away although she would be busy helping Bill and Sophie set up the new clinic and her mother's wedding had to be arranged if only a simple affair at sunset on Cable Beach.

Now Pauline seemed more settled. 'At least she had made peace with Ross and there was hope' she mused as she drifted off to sleep.

Chapter Twelve

Pauline woke with a start looking at her watch, it was 2pm, her mother and David would arrive any minute. She showered quickly and had just finished dressing when they arrived.

"Good trip home love?" Jane asked.

"Mum it was fantastic, wished it would never end. A completely new experience" Pauline enthusiastically replied.

"Sorry about my son, sometimes he is a bit abrasive. Lives a lot on his own, seems to prefer his own company" David informed her.

Pauline jumped to his defence, "Ross is a gentleman David" she replied.

David smiled at Jane, he had been hoping for some time his son would finally meet a girl who understood him and had the spirit to overcome all the difficulties a relationship with him in such isolation would bring. 'What an amazing turn of events if Jane's daughter married my son' he mused 'creating a complete family tie-up'.

David knew however to intervene in any way by either parent, as they both agreed could be fatal and that things must take their own course. Though, smiling, he knew Pauline had more grit and determination than anyone he had ever met. He really admired her.

Pauline had arranged to meet Sophie and Bill at their new clinic and borrowing her mother's car she drove into

Chinatown. Finding the new clinic she whistled when she walked in. Sophie had in a few short days transformed the place, builders busy putting the finishing touches to the reception desk, technicians under Bill's watchful eye setting up the computer system and Sophie fitting curtains and overseeing the setting up of chairs for clients, a busy hive of activity.

Sophie waved as she entered and Bill on seeing Pauline idled over and hugged her, "Come into my office please Pauline I just want a quiet chat" he directed.

Pauline entered his office. It was furnished now and looked very professional. She had to congratulate Sophie who had more talent than she had ever imagined. 'Perhaps' Pauline thought 'many have if given the opportunity to develop it'.

Seated, Bill looked at Pauline and smiled, "Pauline I can never repay you for delivering me Sophie. I promise to always treat her with respect and love" Bill looking serious informed her.

"I know that Bill you are a wonderful man, hopefully one day I may find such happiness" Pauline replied.

"I have a few things to inform you Pauline. Please, I am not trying to interfere but you are a dear friend and I love you. Ross is a different person. His mother passed away when he was young and his father David is a hard business man. Ross always thought he had to prove something to his dad. His life is one of hard work and no play. I know or suspect he is a virgin. As far as women go his skills, as you have learnt are zero. Please forgive us but Sophie passed on what happened including the

127

preg-testing. I will clear that up too, no hand up bum for humans Pauline, just a simple test, so hope that eases your worries there. My suggestion to win Ross is to take the lead. Be strong, if you wait for him to make a move nothing will happen. We have a vested interest. Imagine how happy your mum would be to have you married to Ross and living up here near her and David. I want it also for my lovely Sophie who is afraid you might pack up and leave" Bill sighed.

"Thanks Bill, I must confess I am confused by Ross's signals but admit I am falling in love with him, he is so gentle and quiet. My heart skips a beat when we are together" Pauline replied.

"Okay Pauline, think positive. I would be grateful if you can at least work for me for a few weeks setting up my computer system, both Sophie and I are hopeless and we admit it" Bill smiled.

Sophie knocked entering with three cups of coffee, placing them on the desk. "Hope you're not mad at me Pauline for sharing your phone calls with Bill but you are my very best friend and I just want you to be as happy as I am" Sophie told Pauline bending over and giving her a hug.

"Dearest Sophie, nothing you say or do will ever spoil our friendship, if it was not for you I would still be back in Canberra" Pauline replied.

"I suggest we finish our coffee, pick up some take away on the way home to eat by the pool and have a swim. Remember, we have a wedding tomorrow night!" Bill responded.

"Pauline we are having a day off tomorrow to help set up the wedding feast. A few are coming from all over, so David tells us and your mum will need our support to get ready" Sophie chipped in.

Pauline felt a bit guilty for being so involved in her own situation that she neglected helping her mother. Now she reflected, was the time to think of her Mum and not of her own selfish interests.

Having picked up a bucket of fried chicken on the way home, they undressed and slipped into the cool relaxing water of the pool. Pauline swam a couple of laps finding it very invigorating, soothing away the aches and pains of her cattle yard experience. Reflecting on that experience, so foreign to her, gave her a feeling of triumph knowing she had endured and won. She had really enjoyed herself.

For whatever reason, Pauline never considered it strange but completely normal for the trio to sit sipping wine and eating chicken in the nude. It gave her a sense of freedom and just seemed natural when Jane and David joined the group, themselves nude and armed with more wine and food.

Discussion turned to the wedding and Pauline apologised to her mother for being so thoughtless.

"Well both you girls can come with me to the salon in the morning and help me for the day. We are a bit behind schedule with our wedding plans because of the muster. David is getting the alcohol and we girls the food" Jane informed them.

"Sorry Mum, where are the wedding and reception taking place?" Pauline asked. "The wedding is to be held on an old pearl lugger as we cruise along at sunset on Cable Beach. The reception, with Bill's help, will be right here in the pool area" Jane answered excitedly.

"Oh Mum, that will be so romantic, well done David" Pauline replied.

"Thanks Pauline, I just feel so lucky meeting your wonderful Mum, nothing would be too good for her. Unfortunately though, after the wedding we have to fly to Darwin for a business meeting. To be honest, over it all, but can't heap more onto Ross. He takes his duties so seriously that any extra work would kill him" David explained.

"What Ross needs is a good wife, one to do the books, to take some pressure off him and slow him down a bit" Sophie blurted out making Pauline blush.

"If only!" David sighed, "I am responsible really I have to admit, I made the beast."

"Cheer up you lot, let's not get too reflective on such a wonderful occasion. I have to announce that Sophie and I will be next, she has agreed to marry me" Bill gleefully informed them.

"Okay, double celebration tonight let's drink to all our dreams and aspirations. We've only Pauline to go and I feel something will happen soon" Jane already half tipsy raised her glass, beaming with delight.

Laughter filled the air. Pauline felt as if she was finally home, blacking out the years of regimentation and trying to please her late father, thrilled for her mother's happiness and the love she obviously shared with David.

It would be midnight before they retired to bed. The

happiness was uplifting, even to Pauline nothing seemed impossible. She and Ross would be attending their parents at the wedding and 'hope shines eternal' she thought as she slipped off to sleep.

Rising late Pauline showered and joined her mother and Sophie at the breakfast table chatting, "Hello sleepy one, no stamina?" Jane joked as she greeted her.

"We both gave our man farewell bonks before they left early" Sophie laughed.

"Please Sophie, don't rub it in" Pauline quipped.

"Right girls let's buy a new frock first shall we, then to the hair salon and finally check the food situation for tonight" Jane suggested as they headed to the car.

Arriving at the shopping centre the trio spent some time trying on dresses, choosing body hugging and revealing skimpy black outfits all similar, even finding matching accessories. All nodded in agreement giving the 'thumbs up' to their purchases.

Two hours later they left the salon having ordered the full treatment even down to a Brazilian each.

"Buggered if I know why I'm bothering!" Pauline declared.

"One never knows" Sophie laughed, "think positive Pauline, when in doubt, attack!"

Arriving home with the boot full of parcels the trio set about preparing food for the evening. "How many are coming Mum?" Pauline asked.

"Well only the wedding party is going on the boat but David has asked a few more back here. Lack of information as to how many is a few more, so let's say 'twenty'. Nice little intimate crowd" Jane replied.

"Did you ask anyone Mum?" Pauline queried.

"No, my old life, thank God, is behind me. I know now that those I thought were friends were not real friends, they were mostly bloody users. In fact you two are my best friends and I am proud to admit that you are better than all those put together" Jane replied.

"You know Mum, I agree. Sadly, in all my time in Canberra, Sophie was the only one I could class as a true friend. I proved that myself by nearly getting rooted by her ex" Pauline laughed.

"Hey you two, that part of my life is over, I am a respectable woman now. Hope to have that marriage annulled soon anyway and then I am following you Jane, into married bliss" Sophie advised.

Setting up tables and chairs around the pool area the trio enjoyed a coffee before helping each other dress. David had told them Bill and Ross would meet him at the beach ready for a runabout to pick them up at 5pm and that they should all meet up there.

Jane arranged for a pearl lugger shuttle bus to pick them up at 4.30pm and deliver them to Cable Beach to join the men before all going aboard. She had hatched this plan, quite sure all would imbibe alcohol to enjoy the moment and she sure intended to as well. It was more than a wedding day for her, it was a new life with a man who treated her like a princess. David constantly told her of his affection and nothing ever seemed too much trouble for him when it came to Jane.

Arriving at the beach David stood smiling dressed in

moleskins and western shirt matched by Ross and Bill who all greeted the trio assisting them to the launch waiting to take them out to the pearl lugger.

Ross held back whilst Bill and David swept their two loves up and carried them to the water. Although hesitant Ross picked up Pauline and carried her to the launch, gently placing her on the seat. Pauline swooned as she felt his taught muscles hold her ever so gently, sorry when the small interlude was over but surprised when he sat next to her for the journey out to the pearl lugger bobbing at anchor.

The Celebrant was already on board with another crew member and as the launch arrived they helped the wedding party up and onto the deck. Bill and David guided Sophie and Jane to a seat on the deck of the swaying pearl lugger, holding them around the waist. Again Pauline felt like swooning as Ross followed their lead.

Once seated the crew hoisted the sails although Pauline guessed a motor was assisting as the wind had dropped right out. It was almost silent as the proud old vessel glided along Cable Beach with the sun beginning to settle in the west. The setting was so romantic with the sails flapping in the wind as drinks were handed out by two of the friendly crew. Pauline had never experienced such a magnificent setting. She knew Ross was watching her intently but did not look back at him as she talked to Sophie who was absolutely enthralled and informed Pauline that this was to be her wedding setting too, it was so out of this world.

The Celebrant suggested that as the sun would set in

about half an hour they should perhaps line up on the bow so he could commence the ceremony. Jane and David holding hands exchanged wedding vows, Jane so overwhelmed she began to cry triggering Pauline and Sophie to shed a few tears too as the pearl lugger glided silently along with Cable Beach slipping past. Pauline and Ross witnessed them sign the Marriage Certificate and they all raised their glasses as Bill, holding Sophie by the hand, toasted the happy couple, "I wish two wonderful people a happy life" adding, "may we all have many more wonderful days together and happy times, although this will be hard to surpass, cheers!"

Pauline taking the initiative slipped her small hand inside Ross's, surprised when he gave it a squeeze and smiled at her. Pauline knew this was a wonderful moment for all and its effect on Ross was not unnoticed.

They all stood spellbound as the sun set in a ball and the crew turned the pearl lugger back to base. Pauline stood holding tightly onto Ross wishing the moment would never end. She was totally in love, indeed madly in love and longing for him to embrace and kiss her as David and Bill had done after the toast.

All too soon the cruise was over and Pauline regretted the moment it ended. Ross again helped her into the launch and lifted her gently out when they grounded on the beach. She was disappointed when he did not come on the bus but David explained he had transported them in his vehicle to the launch and would meet up back at Bill's.

As the small coach approached the house Jane exclaimed,

"Bloody hell David a few friends indeed!"

Vehicles stretched to the end of the street on both sides and couples from interstate walked along from nearby resorts. Alighting from the coach Jane and David were swamped with well-wishers, Pauline losing Bill and Sophie as well as her mother and David as they crowded around in the carnival like atmosphere. Pushing her way into the pool area she was amazed at the number of people and at the presents stacked high in one corner, the laughter and mayhem electric.

Pauline however had only one agenda and that was to find Ross, her heart ached for his presence. He had ignited a passion even Pauline was finding hard to come to terms with. She knew only intercourse would quell her fire!

Walking to the end of the street she was bitterly disappointed when she was unable to locate his vehicle. Amongst all the happiness she was desperately miserable. Again she searched all the faces. Her mother was busy meeting David's friends some of whom had come from interstate for the occasion and Sophie was also kept busy as a proud Bill introduced her to David's friends, many he knew also.

Pauline wandered amongst the throng for about an hour. Feeling sad and disillusioned she headed home to her bed next door. Entering the kitchen for a drink she gasped, Ross was seated at the breakfast bar drinking a beer. "Thank you once again Ross. I was heartbroken when you did not show up, why are you so thoughtless?" Pauline asked sobbing.

Ross with the look of a naughty child stood up and

slowly walked to Pauline wrapping his arms around her, "I apologise for all the bad things I have done to you. I know about the food you wanted to cook for me and how brave you were in the cattle yards but to be honest I just do not like big crowds. I am in love with you Pauline and was sitting here getting up the courage to tell you. On the pearl lugger I promised myself to one day soon marry you like Dad married your mum, but now I suppose I have hurt you too much" Ross told her solemnly.

Pauline felt weak and near collapse, "You silly bugger I just couldn't understand it. Since that first day my mind has thought of nothing else but getting you into bed, I am so happy my heart is bursting" she cried.

Bending over, Ross kissed her gently and she responded with passion dragging him to his room. She flung her clothes onto the floor but he was hesitant and not sure what to do so she helped him undress then both entwining fell onto the bed. Pauline pulled him to her, embracing in a passion she had never felt before as his rock hard penis pushed gently into her making her gasp for breath.

Pauline's passion rose within as he slowly slid deep into her and her body shuddered, the feeling both ecstatic and electrifying at the same time. So strong was her want for him she wrapped her small legs around him groaning in pleasure. She felt him shudder as sticky spurts of semen came deep inside her. Still the passion burned as they kissed. Pauline was surprised when she again felt his cock swell slowly and they became lost in pleasure as each rose with every thrust. Pauline reached a crescendo in a mind blowing orgasm that even alarmed her it was so deep and prolonged. She felt as if she was floating in a sea of pleasure. Like insatiable animals they pleasured each other for hours, time and time again, copulating with passion, Pauline having woken a tiger with the staying capacity of a bull. Finally in the early hours of the morning and locked in a tight embrace they drifted off to sleep.

Chapter Thirteen

Jane and David Anderson waved the last of their guests off at 2am and exhausted made their way arm-in-arm to their home. On entering Jane noticed Pauline's little black number in the hallway outside the door of the room Ross used on his infrequent visits. Intrigued she slowly opened Pauline's bedroom door only to find the bed was still made, unused. David had already gone to bed and Jane knew would be waiting to consummate the marriage but unable to control her interest she slowly pushed open Ross's door. A gasp came from her as she smiled with glee when she saw Pauline and Ross naked, still entwined on top of the bed, sleeping peacefully. Jane shed a tear of happiness for Pauline, she really had thought of Ross as 'unwinable'.

Scurrying to her bedroom she whispered to David, "Your lovely son and my daughter are in bed together wrapped in ecstasy, I imagine after a love session."

"Are you kidding me or have my dreams come true?" David quizzed Jane as he dragged her onto the bed in a passionate embrace slipping between her legs, sighing in pleasure as he felt her ready wetness, so inviting. 'This was a truly remarkable day' he thought as he moved into pleasure mode riding Jane, hopeful his son would experience and enjoy the same passion with her daughter.

Pauline woke on daylight busting for a pee and untangled herself from a slumbering Ross to race to the toilet. On the way back she made two coffees and a plate of food to share with Ross who was now awake and looked as concerned as a small child at her absence.

Pauline sat up in bed next to her greatest achievement unable to stop smiling at him. As she fed Ross the cheese and meat cuts she had plundered from the kitchen, a gentle tap came on the door, "Come in" Pauline beckoned.

"We have a plane to catch in an hour, could you two pick up my car at the airport later?" Jane requested grinning at Ross with his head on Pauline's lap tucked under her breasts as she fed him morsels of food.

"Sure Mum, we are having the day at home then back to work Monday for us both" Pauline replied.

"Take care, my two favourite people" Jane replied closing the door.

Neither Pauline nor Ross spoke but sat drinking the coffee and eating the food looking into each other's eyes. Both having sipped the nectar of each other's presence and aroma they had formed a bond so strong it was almost extreme.

Placing the tray on the floor Pauline pulled the sheet from Ross swooning when she saw his erect penis. It was 'beautiful' she thought as she placed her small hands around it, stroking it gently. Placing her mouth over his rising desire she slowly and erotically teased it with her lips delighting in the small gasps of pleasure coming from Ross. Staring at his erect, moist, throbbing member she gently straddled him groaning herself in pleasure as she consumed it, gradually rising up and down its full length rocking from side to side, lost completely in the moment.

She stared into his glazed eyes. Several times just sitting still, then leaning forward and pressing her breast against his heaving chest she gently teased his lips with her tongue before kissing him full on the mouth.

Suddenly like a caged lion breaking free he grabbed her. With a look of wild lust on his face he rolled her over on the bed, parted her legs and in one thrust drove into her like a wild animal. Overcome with passion Pauline's body shuddered, the rising passion making her scream for more as she felt her whole body shake in an uncontrollable orgasm. She felt waves of his semen coming in her as Ross collapsed panting and covered in sweat.

Rolling apart Pauline stared at the ceiling panting too, having reached heights she'd never before experienced. His hand sought hers as they lay in the afterglow on a soaking bed and after what seemed like an eternity Pauline rose and leaning over Ross, whispered, "Promise me we will always be as passionate as in that moment, it felt like an out of body experience".

"I will always try to please you Pauline. Life without you now would be unbearable" Ross replied holding her close for several minutes.

Sharing a long shower and each washing the other gently but so erotically they returned to Pauline's clean bed. Wrapped in each other's arms and forced into absolute abandonment by a passion so great they gave way to their insatiable want for each other.

Many times during the day they enjoyed slow and erotic sex only arising late that evening for food and another shower before returning to the bed. Neither bothered dressing, today was a day of learning how to pleasure each other especially for Ross. His long suppressed unabated sexual feelings now released like a torrent and his most inner desires increased each time he gazed at Pauline. Only small but with big erotic breasts and an intimacy within her that raged like a fire.

Both knew as daylight crept across the room they had jobs to attend to. One final embrace and Ross dressed, watched by Pauline awestruck at his staying ability. She had forgotten how many times he had taken her, more sex than she had in her previous life by many times and loving sex at that, she had reached nirvana.

"I won't be home till after dark. Can you pick up your Mum's car later?" Ross asked, "Perhaps Sophie can drop you off at the airport on the way to work" he suggested.

"Okay but when you go home, Pauline is coming with you!" she replied.

"Honest, Pauline the thought of not having you in my bed of a night is horrific, promise me you will come with me" he begged. "Try and go without me Ross Anderson and watch out" she laughed happily. Pauline now had what she so desperately yearned for her whole life, someone she wanted and who wanted and cared for her too.

Ross gave her a hug and left. Pauline lay glowing for a short time then in a flurry dressed, stripped both beds, washed the sheets all stained with lovemaking, then hung them out to dry just as Sophie rounded the corner.

"Hi Pauline I worried about you the night of the party but your mum filled us in yesterday morning before she left. Wow girl, come on tell me what happened" Sophie beamed.

"Sophie all my wildest dreams have come true. I came home early, shattered after the hand holding on the pearl lugger, searched for Ross and he was sitting here quietly trying to get up confidence to tell me he loved me" Pauline replied glowing with happiness.

"Okay now girls' info Pauline, tell me the nitty gritty details!" Sophie cheekily demanded.

"Truth Sophie, he is a fucking bull. We shagged so many times I lost count, he is unstoppable, a turnaround in less than an hour and I orgasmed nearly every time. I am in heaven" Pauline confessed.

"Rumour mill has it he has a big dick, apparently so!" Sophie chuckled.

"Well it's beautiful and thick but not enormous thank God, just enough to fill me completely and send me into seventh heaven" Pauline remarked.

"Okay Pauline, enough of this, down to business, we have cleaners coming shortly. I will drop you off at the airport to pick up your mum's vehicle. Then it's off to work today for us loose women. Bill needs the clinic system up before Wednesday, he is anxious to open" Sophie informed her.

"How are things going with you Sophie, preggers yet?" Pauline asked as they drove into town.

"No, not through lack of effort though. Must be the hot climate, these buggers up here shag like there is no tomorrow" Sophie quipped.

"Sophie I dream that we can both get pregnant. What a wonderful end to our journey together, both married and pregnant" Pauline confided.

"You know Pauline my annulment will come through later this month and I have been thinking. Would you consider a double wedding?" Sophie asked earnestly.

"Oh Sophie, of course let's share our happy day together" Pauline answered as they pulled up at the airport.

"Done" Sophie beamed giving Pauline the thumbs up as she opened the door of her mother's car. Pauline too felt her heart was bursting. Life was turning out to be a fairytale for all.

As they drove the short distance to Chinatown Pauline immersed herself in setting up programs on the state of the art computer system. Again she became conscious of just how many people so far away imposed stupid and time consuming rules on private enterprise, basically useless but costly and time consuming for those delivering services.

Bill congratulated Pauline and readily agreed to Sophie's suggestion of a double wedding and, as soon as possible he joked. The atmosphere in the surgery was of laughter and friendship, far different from Pauline's previous years of work. Although she missed Ross the day flew by for Pauline and an enjoyable lunch while talking to Bill and Sophie made it special.

Bill in a moment of reflection suggested to both that the wedding be held at the station since it was Ross's life, his obsession and passion. Perhaps to marry his first and one true love in the gardens may please him.

Both Sophie and Pauline agreed planning to marry on a Saturday afternoon, stay overnight and return Sunday to Broome. Bill chuckled as he left the soon to be newlyweds deep in discussion.

Pauline drove home feeling somehow content but longing to be with Ross. She missed him even though it had only been twelve hours and longed for his company, it gave her a sense of security and peace.

Walking in she noticed the little black dress she had worn for her mother's wedding draped over the chair. Picking it up she decided to always keep it as a special memento of when Ross had first kissed her but then decided instead to marry him in it. The garment she felt had brought her one great wish to a happy conclusion.

Pauline covered the dress protectively in an overwrap and hung it in her wardrobe. Showering she changed into a flimsy lace teddy along with the panties she wore for Abdul's seduction. Looking in the mirror she nodded in satisfaction at her reflection.

Setting the table Pauline placed two T-bone steaks in the pan with tomatoes and onion which she knew was one of Ross's favourite meals. With the meal cooking and humming happily Pauline heard Ross arrive so rushed to the door opening it for him. Seeing Pauline he gulped and, dropping his lunch bag, grabbed her, kissing her passionately. He picked her up as she wrapped her legs around him. Closing the door he dropped his shorts and tearing her flimsy panties aside impaled her against the wall bouncing her up and down on his throbbing cock. Turning, still coupled he carried her to the couch and placing her over the arm rode her like a raging bull, both climaxing together, their passion almost frightening as he slipped from her.

Gaining her feet Pauline smiled passing him a beer already on the table waiting, "Wow lover you are amazing, that was incredible" Pauline almost sang.

"I thought of nothing else all day but you Pauline, it is you who is amazing" Ross replied now settling down.

"Have a quick shower love and I will finish dinner" Pauline suggested, still beaming as she picked up her torn panties and threw them in the bin. Must remember she chuckled to herself, no panties when he returns home of an evening!

Pauline was surprised how in her company and alone Ross chatted non-stop. She had entered his world and was somehow now a major part of it. He seemed to have complete confidence in her, in fact he had suggested if possible on Friday that she drive the Winnebago to the station with her belongings and he would fly to her straight from work as the station he was mustering was only an hour's flight from his station.

Pauline agreed, sure the computer setup would be finished and trialled with Bill and Sophie starting to take clients on Wednesday.

Pauline completed her work and the system was in fact working Wednesday when the first patients arrived. Sophie with her outgoing personality suited Bill's practice perfectly. They both worked well as a team and although Pauline felt sad at leaving her work so soon she contemplated no other course, to stay in Broome while Ross returned home to the station was no option. Her course was now set in cement as she waited each night for his return and for them to melt into each other's arms.

Ross shared his dreams and aspirations with her. The station she understood was his life and for their relationship to succeed she must accept this and share with him as a couple the wonderful dream he so passionately lived. They would chat for many hours at a time about the future and she even mentioned once that she was willing to throw her little nest egg into their future plans but he seemed shocked at her suggestion. 'Like father like son' she thought, instilled in his makeup was that a man must provide for his woman so she never mentioned it again.

On the Friday Pauline was already packed and as she dropped Ross off at the hangar cheerfully waved as she pulled out onto the Great Northern Highway on her last big journey alone, she was going home.

Pauline anxious to reach her destination drove until midday before stopping to stretch her legs and snack on some sandwiches she had made. Not bothering to have a hot drink she drank an orange juice and drove on, once again her strong will and determination kicking in arriving home at 4pm. Elated as she stepped from her Winnebago to be met by Colin smiling, "Welcome balls and fanny!" he laughed, "I hoped to see you back again".

"Thanks Colin, mind giving me a hand to move in? Pauline asked blushing.

Without instruction Colin moved her into the master bedroom, news travels fast up here she smiled.

"You really need a housekeeper here Pauline no doubt Ross will have you out on the station working and I have to go soon otherwise I'll end up not leaving" he chuckled.

Pauline contemplated Colin's comment. She did not

need a sexy backpacker in her domain and although she trusted Ross implicitly she could do without any distraction. Then an idea came to her, shuffling through her bag she found the phone number of Margaret her saviour in Esperance, ideal she grinned. Again she entered the office, 'what a shambles' she thought glancing about. Finding the phone Pauline dialled the number and after what seemed an eternity a man answered.

"Hello" he said in a gruff voice.

"Hi, I am Margaret's niece" Pauline lied "Can I speak to her please!"

"She has no bloody niece as far as I know" was the answer.

"Tell her it is Pauline please, she may not remember me" Pauline politely replied.

Pauline heard the phone bang on the bar and voices in the background.

"Hi Pauline, Margaret here how can I help you?" Margaret came on line.

"Margaret do you remember me, can you talk?" Pauline asked.

"Yes lovey, are you okay? Nice to hear from you, no one seems to care about me, first call in years" Margaret replied.

"Margaret listen, I have a job for you. My partner and I run a station, it's isolated but beautiful. We need a cook and housemaid, only two of us mostly, good wages plus free board and food, just thought you might like it, don't mean to intrude." Pauline said shaking with hope.

"Pauline, are you serious? I was belted again last night

147

and I am sick of this shit. You may well have saved my life, it seems like a dream" Margaret replied.

"Good, can you get to an airport and have you any money?" her mind racing, Pauline questioned.

"Jacko the truckie is here. He will be leaving after dinner and heading to Perth. Even he feels sorry for me so I reckon he would help me" Margaret replied.

"Okay go with him, I will phone now and have a ticket waiting at the Qantas reception desk for you, make sure you have some ID" Pauline instructed.

"I will be there. Thanks Pauline I may never again get a chance for a decent life. I have no mobile but will phone you from the airport when I arrive. I have a hundred dollars, plenty enough for food. Thanks darling girl, I will never forget you for this" she replied as the phone clicked.

Pauline phoned Qantas to purchase an open ticket from Perth to Broome as promised. She was happy. She had repaid Margaret and found a good cook in one call.

She then made a call to the airport in Broome, spoke to one of the light plane operators and paid for a charter for Margaret from Broome to the station for when she arrived. Satisfied she hung up and immediately set about filing and tidying up the office, in fact she was still at it when she heard the beating of an approaching helicopter and ran from the office as Ross jumped out. With the rotor blades still winding down he ran to her scooping her off her feet.

"Sorry I was not here to meet you but now will do" he said placing her gently down and kissing her lovingly.

148

"Come on, nice shower first then some food and let's see what comes after that!" he laughed as he pulled her towards the bedroom.

Pauline noticed the passion in his eyes as she undressed. Somehow it gave her a sense of power that he wanted her with such passion and love. For the first time in her life she really felt wanted, loved for who she was and lusted after. Her innermost soul floated in the clouds in pure rapture.

Colin had a meal prepared by the time they appeared again, both flushed. He grinned, 'the old Ross is a goner' he mused, 'although he has a bit of catching up to do but with that little spunk rat it won't take him long'.

When Pauline told Ross the full story about Margaret he did not hesitate to agree that she join them, hoping she would settle as many found the isolation too hard and left for civilisation after only a short period of time. Pauline too was hopeful but knew that beneath her rough exterior Margaret was a caring person who only wanted someone to appreciate her and to feel safe after years of mental and physical abuse at the hands of men who used her for self-gratification.

Margaret duly arrived and settled in with a bang, ordering Colin from her kitchen. The two soon formed a love/hate relationship but strangely Colin never mentioned leaving again and thrived on their togetherness which Pauline hoped would end up in bed. 'Everyone needs someone' was now Pauline's mantra.

For the next few weeks Ross and Pauline spent every day together, working on far flung stretches of the property and many a night, snuggling up in a swag, content and in love.

When the last muster was carried out Sonny and Billy turned up. Sonny was happy to see Pauline back and again stayed in her shadow, watching for danger, giving advice and caring for her. The two formed an unspoken bond of mutual trust and respect, Pauline even laughing at his sense of humour when he was taking the piss out of his own people, a real character.

Sophie rang often as did Jane and all three arranged a weekend double wedding at the station for the following weekend. Pauline having given her a new start in life now had a wonderful friend in Margaret who relished her new position and delighted in the coming event and Pauline's happiness. She would not hear of any caterers being hired and informed Pauline that with Colin's help, since he was now allowed in the kitchen again, she would serve up more than enough food to feed any army.

Chapter Fourteen

As the weekend approached even the shy Ross was eager to marry his one true love. On one of their talks Pauline asked Sophie if it were possible for Bill to confidentially preg-test her. She had had no periods for two months and suspected she was pregnant but dared not hope or tell Ross until she was positive.

Sophie was elated and told her she had tested positive last week but wanted to tell Pauline when she came back, "Two preggers women getting married" Sophie blurted , "how absolutely wonderful."

"Just tell Bill, if he starts lubing up gloves he can forget it!" laughed Pauline.

As usual the bush telegraph hummed, the old Surgeon was marrying a younger woman and Ross, the confirmed bachelor and loner was falling on his sword the same day. No invitations necessary but bring grog!

Pauline kissed Ross bouncing out of bed before he had a chance to have his morning bonk not wanting to have a big red, smelly fanny when Bill examined her later that morning. Showering, she dressed and made her way to the kitchen joining both Colin, seated drinking a coffee and Margaret, singing away with bacon and eggs sizzling in the pan.

Pauline drank a glass of milk but declined the bacon and eggs. Margaret looked at her, "Instinct tells me lovey that my Pauline may be expecting!" "Okay you old bugger you have me, don't tell Ross until I have my test today. Bill is going to do it for me." Pauline beamed, her happiness like a bubbling stream shining in the sun.

Both hugged Pauline, "A baby round here would really bring this place to life" an excited Colin announced.

"You won't be here mate, you are leaving, or so you keep saying" Margaret said with sarcasm.

"You would miss me too much Margaret old girl" Colin laughed.

"Listen Mister Bloody Smarty Pants, I'd miss you like I'd miss a migraine" Margaret replied.

Pauline laughed, "Come on you two, for fuck's sake get in the cot and have a good shag, why put off the inevitable? Then at least we might get some peace."

Colin and Margaret blushed, both knowing Pauline was right. Now their shield had collapsed Pauline saw the hungry looks they gave each other and knew tonight their relationship would be consummated sexually.

Pauline heard the phone ring and running to the office picked it up. It was her mother just leaving Katherine enquiring if she wanted anything before they left. Pauline advised that all was in order and that Sophie had forwarded drinks and a heap of food in preparation last week. All that remained was for them to travel safely and arrive in good time.

Ross skulked about already worried about the coming event trying not to show his panic at the converging crowd. He knew his father and Bill had many friends who would want to attend, it was a good excuse in this part of the country for a get-together and major piss-up.

Pauline was seated under a flame tree in the garden now coming back to life with both Margaret's and Colin's help. Staring at the river below she somehow saw what Ross loved about this country, huge and unforgiving but wild and magnificent. She felt her tummy and hoped the child she was carrying had the same passion for it as his father and she did. To even contemplate living anywhere but here in their own piece of paradise was now not an option she would consider. 'Yes' she mused, 'who would have thought!'

Her concentration was broken by an approaching plane circling overhead before lining up the runway below. Pauline glanced at her watch, 'It was only midday for God's sake' she thought, then shook her head, 'but this is the Kimberleys' as another appeared high above waiting to land.

Colin had drinks and nibbles set up in an old tack room and Pauline started to greet her guests who after a bit of back slapping and passing presents to her started into the well-stocked bar as another helicopter thundered overhead. From here on in Pauline's day became a dream, vehicles arriving, planes and choppers screaming overhead, people milling about laughing and shaking her hand so violently she thought her arm would be dislocated.

Pauline watched her beloved Ross trying to look confident as he met the arriving throng and sidling up next to him gave him a peck on the cheek, "I promise my love after this day you are mine all to myself, stay strong for me, tonight you will make love to your wife" she whispered.

Ross smiled, "I'd go through this a thousand times for

you Pauline" he replied as another visitor arrived shaking their hands and congratulating them both.

Sophie and Bill arrived for the special occasion, having hired a plane and pilot. The company even arranged for the pilot to stay with the plane and take the happy couple back later the next day.

Sophie pulled Pauline to the side, "Here quick go and pee in this for me, just have to know!" Sophie whispered excitedly.

"Is it that simple, no fanny inspection?" Pauline asked.

"A bit worried about you wanting my Bill to check your fanny Pauline. No, not necessary" Sophie laughed.

Sophie waited outside the bathroom while Pauline filled the container then placing a strip in the urine Sophie laughed with glee, "Definitely up the spout Pauline. Bill said to come in later for a proper check-up, but you show positive!"

Pauline, now glowing, found it impossible to wait any longer. She found Ross baled up by several men and women mostly questioning him about her. Grabbing him by the arm she joked to the watching crowd, "Just need my husband-to-be for a few minutes, have a small matter to attend to in the kitchen!"

Once away from the crowd Pauline held him by the hand looking into his beautiful big confused eyes she said, "Ross my love, afraid to tell you but the woman you are marrying today is two month's pregnant with your child".

Ross hugged her tightly. She saw a small tear run down his cheek, so overcome he did not reply. A few months ago he'd never have thought something like this would happen in his life, but now he had a family.

"Thank you Pauline, now we will have a real family. This place will really come to life, how lucky am I!" he replied gaining his composure.

After sharing the news they both returned to the guests and now even Ross joined in the rejoicing. David and Jane arrived and they were both elated when Pauline told them the news that they would be grandparents. David shook his head at the change in his life Jane had given him. Just a drink with a lonely lady, 'thank the fuck for Timbuktu' he laughed to himself.

Pauline remembered the afternoon as being a haze of happy faces, introductions by people she had never heard of, groups standing laughing and talking, exchanging jokes and news, trying to play the good host. She sought out Ross giving him support, aware that this was his personal space now invaded by well-meaning friends. She too longed for the return of tranquility and the peace she had so far shared with Ross, her friend Margaret and old Colin.

Pauline stood under her favourite tree, a beautiful African Flame Tree, now covered in flowers. Here she had chosen to be married. Gazing at the river below and the mountain range beyond, she looked forward to the rains not far away when the raging river would isolate them for months, with access only by air Ross informed her. Already they had stocked up on fuel and supplies in the store and Pauline relished the time ahead with Ross, dreaming in such isolation of being divorced from the real world, alone and in love.

She was brought back to the reality of the day when

her mother looking fussed approached, "Come on Pauline time to freshen up, the ceremony is in half an hour, where the hell is Sophie?" Jane questioned sounding concerned.

"Find Bill Mum and you'll find Sophie. I will go shower and change. Thanks Mum, can you believe what has happened to us?" Pauline replied hugging her Mum.

"No dear, not in my wildest dreams. Strange how the real person can be trapped because of circumstances, we are the lucky ones, we had an opportunity to fly free but many never get the chance we stumbled on. Grab it Pauline, live it, fly high and free, we have two wonderful men. New horizons await you, motherhood and family, wonderful friends and a life of bliss far removed from a sick world" Jane sobbed, a tear running down her cheek.

"True Mum I would not even know what is going on in the world, no newspapers here and we seem not to have time to watch TV, to be frank do not even miss it" Pauline told her heading to the homestead through a mass of people.

Showering she applied her makeup with Margaret's help and although against tradition pulled on her black skimpy little number, her good luck dress. Sophie arrived, "Shit, sorry Pauline, I was so wrapped up in meeting people I lost track of the time. How the hell do they all know us when we've never heard of most of them?" Sophie quizzed jumping into the shower.

"Bush telegraph!" Margaret yelled back.

By the time both made it to the ceremony they were five minutes late. Bill and Ross stood under the flame tree waiting in anticipation having both chosen David and Jane as attendants and witnesses.

As if on-queue several eagles circled above when the ceremony started. After the formalities both couples exchanged kisses and the crowd erupted. The circle of life continued. Far from the big cities, here in the wilderness and isolation, two couples from such different backgrounds each joined together in the age old tradition of marriage.

Bill who had agreed to save shy Ross the embarrassment of a speech raised his hand for quiet and took the microphone.

"On behalf of both grooms I sincerely thank you for making so much effort to join us today on this happy occasion, free grog and food of course may have helped. Thanks to you all sincerely. We in the bush are known for our friendships and hospitality and of course the bush telegraph. I know you will all be happy with our choices. When you get to know Pauline and Sophie you will love them both as we do."

"Now you may wonder if we are planning a family. Well in true tradition regarding the birth of the first child, both ours will be delivered in about six months. In my particular case this may come as a surprise but be assured we oldies can tell you 'An old fiddle plays a sweet tune'." Bill added, sitting down to a thunderous applause of clapping, yelling and cat-calling.

David Anderson then stepped to the microphone, "I reiterate Bill's words and thank you once again. We Andersons of late seem to be getting married on a regular basis. I have known Sophie and Pauline for some months now and I am proud to welcome Pauline as a member of my family. An extraordinary individual who I personally observed in her first foray into the pastoral industry get zapped with a prodder, pissed on, nearly trampled by mickey bulls and each time brushed herself off and stood tall continuing without complaint proving to be one tough little individual. I can understand why my bachelor son fell in love with such a feisty woman. Knowing her mother so well I can confirm these are two very special women.

Now our Sophie! No wonder my neighbour and lifelong friend Bill is all smiles, dirty old bugger, not a man here wouldn't envy him. A remarkable friend of Pauline's and my wife, I am proud to also call Sophie my friend.

There is no man happier with the sparkle, excitement and energy Pauline and Jane have bought into his life than the one who stands before you tonight. Enjoy the night and travel home safely tomorrow my friends. Finally, live, love, laugh and take your Viagra!" David sat down to thunderous applause.

"One joke David, come on" someone yelled from the crowd followed by loud clapping.

"Okay my jokes are mainly famous for being bad but here goes!" and again stood up still with microphone in hand. "Don't actually know if this is true but a friend from NSW emailed it to me yesterday."

"A group of farmers were having a meeting with a politician and some greens about dingoes and wild dogs causing havoc amongst the sheep, killing dozens a night.

Now the politician present, no names but he has

a bald head and used to be in a band, gets up and advises, on behalf of the panel, that a more humane way to get rid of the dingoes and wild dogs than trapping and shooting them would be to catch the males and castrate them.

Deadly silence came over the meeting. Most present in disbelief that this lot actually helped run the county. Then one old wag at the back of the hall stands up and says, 'They're not fucking the sheep, they're eating them'.

With that the farmers burst into laughter and the red-faced greenies and polly exited the stage to an uproarious round of applause. "

David took a bow as again thunderous applause erupts, the band on standby strikes up, drinks flow, old friends catch up and new relationships are formed. Campfires twinkle in the night, tents spring up and swags are unrolled and the long night of celebration begins as only the north can deliver. No drunken fights, no drugs, no police and ambulances, just friends letting their hair down. Hard tough men and women enjoying a rare opportunity to enjoy each other's company, catch up on gossip, get drunk and if lucky, get laid.

It would be 2am before Ross and Pauline slip from the now boisterous party. Closing their bedroom door both undress, sliding under the sheets. Now with the wet approaching it is still muggy and the fan swirls overhead as they lock in an embrace. Somehow both are so tired and happy just to have each other close after such a long and tiring day is sufficient. Mr and Mrs Ross Anderson fall off to sleep, Ross with his large hand gently rubbing Pauline's stomach, already showing a small bump.

Chapter Fifteen

Pauline was woken by the sound of Margaret quietly entering the room and placing a breakfast tray on the bedside table.

"Thanks Margaret what a lovely surprise" Pauline told her as rubbing her eyes she looked at the clock, it was 9am.

"Special breakfast for special people" Margaret smiled.

"Did someone else have a special night also?" Pauline asked.

"At my age one does not boast about such things but, since you ask, I got a good 'rogering' as you say Pauline" Margaret laughed and left, quietly closing the door.

Slipping silently from the bed Pauline went to the toilet. Ross was waking up as she returned. "Good morning Mrs Anderson" he quipped.

"How are you feeling today Mr Anderson?" Pauline replied sliding beneath the sheets.

"Let me show you just how I feel Mrs Anderson!" he replied gently locking her in an embrace, kissing her with tenderness and running his hand down to her crotch. She responded by grabbing and stroking his rock hard penis. As he slid over on top raising above her on his elbows she noticed, no doubt because of her pregnancy, that he was ever so gentle as he entered her slowly, both climaxing after what seemed an eternity of lovemaking.

Glancing again at the clock Pauline noticed she had been lost in pure pleasure for more than half an hour and only then remembered the breakfast tray.

"Ross Anderson you have ruined the lovely surprise Margaret delivered earlier" Pauline scolded him, as she placed the tray between them.

Both enjoyed the breakfast of pancakes and yogurt, even more so when Ross placing some of the yogurt playfully on her nipples sucked it off rolling his tongue around them while looking into her eyes like a naughty child.

"You can spoil breakfast any time you like Mr Anderson, if you repeat this morning's performance" she giggled.

Showering together they both dressed and strolling onto the veranda Pauline gasped as her garden looked like a war zone, bottles and cans everywhere. A few people strolled about, many lay in swags. Margaret and Colin had coffee and pancakes going in the tack room. A few sick looking clients swallowed the coffee but only picked at the pancakes.

David Anderson joined them, "Don't worry Pauline when they sober up later and rise from the dead be assured they will all chip in and clean up. The buggers love a good party" he informed her.

"No problems David it just caught me by surprise, have you seen Bill and Sophie?" Pauline asked as her mother approached looking a bit seedy.

"Old Bill got a bit carried away last night with the celebrations, all his old mates insisting on having a drink with him, so poor Bill, if I were to take an educated guess, is still in bed with Sophie fussing over him" David chuckled, holding his own head as Jane passed him a horrible looking concoction.

Ross sat with his parents on the porch gazing at the carnage below, some hardy ones still propping up the bar. Pauline shook her head in amazement as she went inside to check on Sophie.

Tapping on her door she entered. Sophie was sitting up in bed with a snoring Bill beside her. Pauline sat down on the other side and they held hands. "We are two lucky buggers Sophie, can you believe last night?" Pauline queried.

"Well it was a hoot but old Sophie thought at least on her wedding night her husband may want a good root" Sophie sniffed looking over at the snoring Bill.

"Poor Bill he was pretty much coerced into having too many drinks but he was one happy man" Pauline replied.

"Still I bet you got a bit Pauline" Sophie whined.

"Well last night 'no' but before we had breakfast 'yes', it was so romantic" Pauline replied recalling the encounter.

"Come on Sophie, let's have a coffee in the kitchen, I'll make you breakfast. Margaret and Colin are down at the tack room feeding the hordes" Pauline said as she dragged her friend from the bed.

Seated alone in the kitchen Sophie returned to her old self, accepting that it was because he was so happy that Bill had entered into the celebrations with a little too much gusto. Pauline goaded her to forgive him and both girls made him up a nice breakfast tray and some very strong coffee.

Sophie returned to the bedroom happily carrying the tray and neither of them appeared until 4pm at which time Sophie gave Pauline the 'thumbs up' as they boarded the aircraft on the return to Broome.

To her surprise Pauline found the gardens being slowly cleaned up under David's guidance. Cars were driven off and planes lifted into the air and by evening Pauline found herself once again the mistress of an orderly station. Even Jane and David had to leave despite her wanting them to stay another night but unfortunately, David informed her, he had a business meeting the next day in Broome.

Pauline and Ross stood on the veranda watching the last guests fly into the sunset, turning she said to him, "Paradise reclaimed darling, let's get an early night, for tomorrow we return to the real world."

"You are my real world Pauline but yes I am tired, a stressful job, this getting married!" Ross replied with a grin as they made their way to the bedroom.

The following morning after breakfast, picking up the lunch basket made by faithful Margaret, Pauline and Ross headed out to far flung reaches of the station repairing fences and bores as the approaching wet brought a crescendo of thunder in the distant hills and gullies. Dark clouds boiled overhead as they worked in tandem, very little conversation flowing between them, it was not part of their makeup, Pauline because of her years keeping quiet so as not to offend her father and Ross because he chose to work in isolation. As the infant grew inside Pauline she gained pleasure from the simple smiles they exchanged as they spent their days together deliriously happy in the strength they drew from each other and perfectly content in their own little world. Pauline too grew more attached to the harsh country she now felt a part of and to the magnificence of its raw beauty.

The surrounds she and Ross travelled were amongst one of the oldest landscapes on the planet and she reasoned that they during their time here, just as that of past owners, would leave little if any footprints. She shuddered at the thought of her beloved mountain ranges ever being blown apart and levelled because of man's insatiable quest for money.

When the first seasonal storms hit they became isolated as the river roared into action and torrents of water came crashing below. Pauline and Margaret often sat on the veranda watching, overawed at nature's power.

Ross suggested to Pauline now heavily pregnant that over the next few days they take the chopper to Broome and await the birth. She would have preferred to leave it to the last minute but at the goading of Bill and Ross relented, sorry to have to leave her safe haven. Pauline accepted too Margaret's advice that if complications arose she needed to be near proper medical facilities.

On a clear, sunny morning Pauline and Ross rose into the air for a direct flight to Broome. Pauline felt a little sad as she waved to Margaret and Colin blowing kisses from below. She would miss them both, they had become very close to her and Ross, almost like family.

Again Pauline, spellbound as they skimmed along, this time taking no diversions, straight towards Broome, wondered how many in their lives would experience the majestic nature of what Australia had to offer in the far flung reaches of the north, fearful of it being destroyed in the name of greed. The vista below made her reflect on just how insignificant humanity was in the greater picture.

As they rose over the mountain range she so often gazed at she asked, "What is that range called Ross? "I love it so much, it gives me a wonderfully peaceful and tranquil feeling" she added.

"It's 'Mount Anderson' named after my ancestor. The small one to the west is unnamed so Dad and I plan to have it officially named 'Mount Pauline' in your honour for the passion you have brought into our lives, especially into mine" he replied.

Pauline could not answer, she was choked up. Knowing the absolute love Ross had for the place, to honour her in such a way rendered her speechless.

Finally she spoke, "Why?" she asked sobbing.

"Because you silly old thing, you are just so special you've brought new life to the station. Since you arrived things have changed, you found Margaret and you've added a real purpose to my life. Great things warrant special treatment and to be rewarded. You deserve it" Ross replied also a bit teary. Pauline knew such a touching statement from him came from the heart. Holding her tummy Pauline just shook her head, her old life now seemed lost in the mists of time as though she had passed away and entered heaven. Almost surreal now she watched the green desert bursting into life, renewed by the changing of seasons forever marching on and here she was about to give life to a baby, fathered by a man she'd never even in her wildest dreams thought existed.

As they approached the hangar menacing clouds boiled to the west and gushes of moist air hit Pauline. Carrying only a shoulder bag because of weight constraints Ross assisted her from the helicopter. Jane waiting in the Landcruiser smiled as they approached fussing over Pauline who complained she personally felt like a beached whale.

Pauline was grateful to finally sit in a comfortable chair and spread out. The news Ross had told her about 'Mount Pauline' seemed to have drained her emotions. Her mother was a little upset at Ross for telling her as it was supposed to be a surprise on her trip home after the birth but proudly showed Pauline the signs that had been made only days before.

Ross looked sheepishly. 'Poor old Ross' she thought smiling, 'so honest he was unable to keep a secret from her, had just blurted it out'.

Sophie also heavily pregnant waddled over and she and Jane paraded the baby clothing and bassinet they had purchased for Pauline. The men retired to the kitchen to enjoy a cold beer.

Pauline and Sophie so excited about their coming deliveries both agreed the sooner the better 'but unfortunately' Sophie thought 'she had a few more weeks than Pauline' who hoped to give birth in two weeks. With an appointment to visit the delivering doctor arranged for 10am in the morning Pauline retired early under strict instructions from Jane.

David and Bill planned to take Ross away for the day knowing he would be like a caged lion if restricted to the house. Since Pauline wanted a Landcruiser, knowing the ute would be a bit crushed with a baby in a bassinet, part of the time would be spent searching the second hand yards in Broome. Jane would bring it in after the wet when the roads opened.

Pauline, although not really wanting one at present, conceded that it would be something to distract a nervous Ross, and David considered that fitting a baby seat even so soon would fill in his time, sure that he would find other repairs or modifications to keep him occupied.

Pauline after living on the station and with the mountain they all now called 'Mount Pauline' found Broome boring. Even trips to the shops did not impress her, she felt happier in her shorts and T-shirt working with Ross on the station.

After three more long weeks Pauline woke with the first of her pains and gently woke Ross. For the first time since she had known him he lost his cool, racing around unable to find his keys, clothes or anything. He woke David and Jane who calmly loaded Pauline into the car for the short dash to the hospital having phoned ahead. Nurses were waiting out front and assisted Pauline into a wheelchair as Sophie and Bill arrived and just as Ross raced in half dressed and in a complete panic.

"Okay Ross, not much we can do here let's go to the waiting room and let the experts do their job" Bill soothingly told Ross.

"Bill, I want to see my baby born" Ross replied.

"Shit, have you told Pauline?" Bill asked.

"No but she would not mind" Ross answered.

"Hold on I'll go and ask" Bill told him.

Bill soon returned, "Pauline said a big yes and cried" Bill laughed telling Ross "come on let's get you suited up and in with your wife, might not be pretty though!"

Ross followed Bill as they disappeared into the birthing room while Sophie in her dressing gown joined David and an anxious Jane in the waiting room.

At 5am Pauline gave birth to a bouncing baby boy. When announcing the news to those who all waited anxiously the delivering doctor added "mother fine, father not doing so well, he is an emotional bloody wreck so much for a tough station owner!"

Shortly after the birth Pauline was sitting up in bed in the post delivery room holding her baby son, her face shining with happiness while Ross sat slumped in the chair, head between his hands.

"Hi guys" a beaming Pauline quipped, "don't worry about poor old Ross, he had a much harder time than I did."

Sophie laughed, "God Ross you look like shit, what happened?"

"It was awful, never putting my Pauline through that again, I nearly fainted and I've got a headache for the first time in my life. God she was brave" Ross replied. Even Pauline laughed as everyone congratulated the couple.

In his present state Ross was of no help, perhaps even a hindrance to Pauline and it was obvious she needed some rest so it was suggested he go home with them for breakfast and a shower before coming back. Of course nothing would have upset an exhausted Pauline now, with the infant suckling on her ample breasts, the glow of motherhood plain for all to see.

Having agreed, and helped by David to the car, Ross was in such an emotional state Bill prescribed a strong calmative for him. Rarely had he seen such a display of emotion from a new father. On the way home Ross admitted he was in awe of his wife, her bravery was indisputable. He would even view sex in a different way he blurted out, the others silently laughing at his emotional state.

Arriving home Bill gave Ross a tablet and he lay down dropping off to sleep, emotionally and mentally drained. Meanwhile back at the hospital Pauline enjoyed breakfast as the baby slept peacefully next to her. Worried, she phoned to see if Ross was okay and much to the amusement of all was informed it would take him weeks to recover from the birth.

Pauline came home the following day to the delight of Ross but the doctor suggested she stay in Broome for a couple of weeks if possible. With the station cut off and work impossible apart from the workshop and station confines all agreed plus Pauline did not want to return until Sophie had given birth.

Jane and Sophie spent all day with Pauline helping and admiring the baby. Pauline insisted on calling her son 'Ross' after his father and no one wanted to argue with her so 'Ross David Anderson' was accepted by all. Exactly two weeks later the phone rang at 10pm. It was Bill to tell them Sophie was on the way to hospital. Without hesitation David, Jane, Ross, Pauline and baby packed into the car and headed to the hospital prepared to wait until Sophie gave birth and to support first time father Bill who fussed about until Sophie ordered him from the delivery room.

A long night ensued until at daybreak with Pauline half asleep and feeding baby Ross, a doctor informed Bill he was the proud father of a little girl and that both mother and baby were fine.

The post delivery room was now full of smiling faces as Sophie, just as Pauline had done, was sitting up in bed absolutely beaming.

Sorry I was so long, lucky bugger Pauline it took me two hours longer" Sophie smiling told them.

Bill held up his daughter and no prouder man existed at that time.

"Enjoy her Bill, one is enough for Sophie, getting preggers is okay but stuff that, my fanny will never be the same again!" Sophie quipped.

'Trust Sophie to say that', Pauline thought, happy for her friend. When everyone had offered their congratulations Bill suggested they leave her alone to rest, it had been a difficult birth.

Arriving home they all went back to bed, Pauline holding her son as he suckled her breast. Ross looked at the pair in wonderment, a feeling of absolute love came over him each time he watched his wife and son.

Sophie arrived home two days later and Ross became anxious to go home, the wet was soon ending and he had repairs to the cattle yards to attend to plus Pauline worried about Margaret despite her constantly telling her to stay as long as necessary. She 'hadn't killed Colin yet' she often said laughingly.

Sophie, Bill and baby along with Jane and David waved the little helicopter away as it rose into the clear Kimberley sky. Ross had tied the bassinet onto a skid and Jane had loaded the rest into the Landcruiser she was to deliver to the station when the roads reopened.

Margaret and Colin waited by the pad waving madly as the little family landed, even Pauline was grateful to be home. She was homesick for the station and passing the baby to Margaret sighed with relief as she stepped onto the cement landing, she was finally home.

Pauline followed Margaret as Ross and Colin removed the bassinet and took it to the bedroom. Ross David Anderson had slept through the trip unaware as he was placed in the bassinet that his homecoming had been a bit unorthodox.

Colin was pleased to inform them nothing of any consequence had happened in their absence and he had started welding repairs on the cattle yards. After lunch accompanied by Pauline back in shorts, the two men made their way to the cattle yards working away together as if nothing had happened. Margaret lovingly watched over the sleeping infant.

Chapter Sixteen

Time again sped by, the road opened and Jane and David arrived along with Bill, Sophie and baby Rachael. Pauline was glad to have the Landcruiser and the supply of baby clothes. It was also good to spend time with Jane and Sophie. Working long hours with Colin and Ross did not afford much chat and Margaret seemed only interested in the baby, he had become her passion.

Sophie and Bill left on the Monday he had a clinic to run still. As they drove off Sophie waved to Pauline. They had shared so much and she really missed her but each evening they exchanged news. It was a highlight of Pauline's day, and no matter what, Sophie always made her feel good.

Again the muster started, long hours in the yards. Pauline enjoyed it especially her banter with Sonny and Billy. She was happy when Sonny asked her and Ross if he could come and live on the station with his wife. The community he told them was getting bad, fighting and drink were making it impossible, the young ones he said were out of control.

Pauline was overjoyed and immediately Jane and Margaret set about cleaning up the old workers' cottage and painting some of the rooms.

The following week Sonny returned with Mona and they settled in. Mona proved to be a good cook and Margaret and she struck up a real friendship babysitting and running the kitchen.

Pauline and Sonny now shot and bush-dressed cattle for the station adding the odd bush turkey to Sonny's menu, he loved them. Much banter took place about their shooting abilities and a strong competition between the two arose over picking off wild dogs, many of which killed several calves every season.

Sonny soon proved to be a good vegetable gardener, every night working until dusk tending a growing garden. Assisted by Colin soon the station became self-sufficient in fresh vegetables. Sonny also supplied fresh fish for the table. He had blended into station life in only a few short weeks.

Once again the muster came to an end and with it another season, as the wet approached. Pauline and Ross headed off every day after she had breastfed their son. Her bond with Ross was iron clad the two becoming inseparable working as a team, even spending evenings in the office catching up on paperwork, spending every moment together. Neither seemed to have any wish to leave the station it was either Margaret and Colin or Sonny and Mona who travelled to town for supplies. Ross and Pauline showed no inclination to go beyond the boundaries of Mount Pauline, now well accepted by all as the legitimate name of the mountain named in her honour.

Three years passed and the seasons came and went, Pauline proudly watching her son running out to greet them when they returned each night, Ross scooping him up. On some occasions now he came with them checking fences. Pauline and Ross had agreed to home school him for his early years but Sophie insisted that later he should live in Broome with them and attend school. Pauline dreaded the time her little family would have to be broken up. She worried too about reports in the few newspapers she read, about a world where there were drug cheats in sport, corrupt politicians and even corrupt priests and pedophiles in the Vatican. No wonder the young are drinking, out of control and lost with no one to look up to. She was worried almost afraid to expose her son to the outside world but deep in her heart she knew it would be unfair as a parent to keep him in ignorance here in her private utopia.

During one of her talks with Sophie, who was never backward in coming forward, she as usual wanted to know how Pauline's sex life was. Hers, she reported, had slowed to twice a week. Pauline had to admit hers had not slowed and seemingly Ross was making up for lost time. His passion, she reported, had not waned. Twice a night, each bedtime and morning he wanted his ride. In their relationship she was slowing down not Ross, she told an envious Sophie.

Pauline's mother and indeed David expressed concern to Pauline about their isolated lifestyle. Pauline assured them they had all they needed here, bonded together in their own sanctuary, totally at peace and content in each other's company. They suggested then that Pauline sell the Winnebago but she simply replied, "The 'Winny' is part of my life, it delivered me here and I owe it. I take it for a run monthly and Colin keeps it clean and changes the oil yearly. Along with my little black dress, the 'Winny' will remain with me for the rest of my life" she assured them.

Knowing Pauline's stubbornness, they both changed the subject. Pauline had found her niche in life and, unlike before, she felt wanted by a worthy husband who worshipped her and a growing son, her life here was complete. Sophie better understood Pauline and fiercely supported her when others voiced concern pointing out Pauline was happy and content in her own little world and that material possessions and wealth did not even appear on her radar suggesting the world would be a better place if only more could be so happy.

Standing in the back of the bull catcher, holding her son, Pauline watched Ross circling the river below trying to dislodge the last of the old mickey bulls.

It was agreed they rid the herd of all the old shorthorn cross bulls and introduce new blood in the form of the larger Brahman cattle. To save money this season they had not hired an extra chopper and trying to muster all the old bulls was a daunting task with one helicopter.

Pauline in one of her mad moments decided she must learn to fly and become a muster pilot herself if she was to really play her part. 'Why should Ross' she thought 'have to face all the danger flying in the dead zone' as it was known in the muster pilot world, one mistake and bingo very few survived. Instead of her just watching, it made so much more sense for the two of them to share the flying.

Ross eventually gave up as the animals either simply turned every time and lodged in the thick clumps of bush or just would not come out. Pauline radioed Ross begging him to give up and bring in the mob already mustered, being held by Colin and Sonny slowly moving them towards the yards led by old cows who knew the procedure from previous seasons. Ross broke off to her delight and strapping her son in she joined the mob taking up her position on the flank, as always watching for the cheeky ones continually looking to break into open country.

Slamming the gate shut Ross wheeled around and headed back to the station, they would give the cattle a day to settle before drafting. Pauline and the crew followed. Now on a mission she went straight to the office and by evening owned her own helicopter, a new Robison and had booked in to do a course with Grant, a muster operator in Broome. Even though she had not left the station in three seasons, this 'wet' she would live in Broome hopeful that Ross would also take a break and wait until she was qualified before mustering again.

That evening alone in bed, the last of the cattle having been drafted and loaded, she informed a shocked Ross of her plans.

"Good God Pauline, are you sure?" he asked in surprise.

"Yes Ross this will put me on equal terms with you and also make mustering easier and faster. We work well together now and this would be the last step to gender equality" Pauline laughed.

On reflection Ross thought 'why not, other women work in the industry?' "One last question then, how can we pay for the new chopper?" he enquired, knowing any argument was a waste of time, but money was tight and he wondered what plan she had come up with.

"Well Ross I did work for sixteen years and Dad left me the house in Canberra. I was a saver and when I sold the house I invested all the money. My only big spend was the Winnebago but even so I had more than enough to pay for the helicopter. In fact I already own it and it is being delivered to Broome next week" she informed Ross who just stared at her with a smile on his face.

"Pauline nothing will ever surprise me about what you can do or what you come up with. I know you will get your Licence and excel. As Dad has always told me, you are one special girl" Ross replied.

"Your dad is a wise man Ross Anderson, now next Tuesday we will take the Winny and head to Broome. I have told no one so let's surprise them they might get a shock when us old hermits turn up!" Pauline informed Ross who was still shaking his head.

Five days later Sophie returned from work to find the Winnebago parked next door on the lawn. Running next door, carrying an excited Rachael, Sophie burst in to find Pauline, Ross and Ross Jnr sitting at the kitchen bench. Sophie fired questions at them both, amazed that after all this time they had actually come to town. When Pauline told her the plan Sophie was gob smacked.

"Pauline you are amazing what next, when do you start?"

"In the morning, the helicopter is here, come on Sophie come with me to see it, Ross might take it for a lap" Pauline full of excitement replied.

"Do Jane and David know? Sophie asked.

"Hell no, they are coming down in three weeks so I

hope to be flying solo by then" Pauline replied.

"Steady Sophie you have to do your practical first and pass a medical test" Ross broke in.

"Mere formalities Ross" Pauline countered, her determination switch on 'high'.

Sophie and Ross looked at each other both aware the only course for them was to go along with Pauline and support her knowing that once she makes a decision you either agree or shut up.

Sophie drove to the helicopter hangar outside town home to the muster business now finished for the season. Maintenance was under way and it was down time for tired pilots for a few months until next season.

Pulling up beside the hangar Pauline knew her new white sparkling machine straight away. 'It was magnificent' she thought, envisaging herself sweeping over the landscape bringing in cattle in tandem with Ross. She was inspired when the children were shown Pauline's new toy.

Ross relented and checking the aircraft found it full of fuel ready for Pauline's upcoming lessons. Both strapped in and Sophie stood with the children watching Ross climb steadily into the air sweeping out of sight before gliding in and landing. Pauline jumped out clapping, she was thrilled. So was Ross, surprised at the new technology and ease of control. Certainly a big difference he told them from the earlier Bell helicopters.

Pauline was eagerly waiting in the office for Grant her instructor the following morning, having obtained her medical certificate with a shocked Bill's assistance the evening before. Grant soon recognised Pauline Anderson as being slightly different from his previous students, confident as she sailed through the theory part of the course and even on her first flight he informed Ross she was a natural. Pauline had a feel for the little machine. She waited anxiously for her instructor weather permitting, every day doing the maximum hours allowed so as to gain the hours required to obtain a Muster Licence. Pauline attacked every test and skill with a vengeance, to her, failure was not an option. Although other husband and wife muster pilot teams existed, Grant readily admitted that nobody he knew had the approach of one Pauline Anderson.

David and Jane arrived late one evening surprised to see the house lights on and the Winnebago parked on the front lawn. Both thinking something terrible had happened they burst into the house only to see Ross nursing Ross Jnr on his knee and Pauline busy cooking dinner.

"What has happened?" Jane blurted out.

"Well Jane, our intrepid Pauline bought herself a helicopter and has almost qualified as a Muster Pilot and a bloody good one at that, she wanted to surprise you both" Ross told her grinning.

"Bloody hell Pauline, you are one amazing woman! Nothing from here on in will ever surprise me in the future. Little did I know when I first met you that one day you would be married to my son, give me a grandchild and muster the station with him in your own helicopter" David laughed shaking his head.

"Strange you are both here, we had decided to fly in next week and share some news with you both anyway, so let me regain my composure or better still, David can tell you both" Jane told them.

"No big deal really, we've both agreed to sell all my business interests and the house in Darwin and come down here full time to spend more time with you guys, especially since we now have a grandson. Time flies by and to be frank age is catching up. You guys will never leave the station and under the present political system I am sick of the bureaucracy. The nation's debt is ballooning and no one cares, personally I am over it" David informed them.

"Mum that is great news and David, I do understand, really I do! We live closeted from the real world on the station and if it had not been for my desire to obtain a Licence I would never have felt a need to leave" Pauline replied.

"If it is okay with you Ross and with Pauline we would like to spend a fair bit of time on the station. I thought, to occupy us both, of setting up a couple of paddocks and growing sorghum for the cattle. I have been studying irrigation south of Darwin. The station has plenty of water with the river and we can pump from that again. We don't want to impose but would love to help out" David informed them both.

"Dad, best news yet, strange I had thought of that but never had the cash or the time" Ross responded and Pauline chipped in beaming, "Well Mum, looks like we are together again!"

Pauline knew David and Jane had made their decision in the hope Ross Jnr would inherit a legacy and continue the family tradition of raising cattle. Despite David having branched into other fields his real interest was to see the station continue and prosper.

On a clear sunny morning as day was breaking, a Winnebago and two vehicles sat parked near the helipads upon which two helicopters were sitting ready for departure.

Sophie with Bill, holding Rachael, bid a fond farewell to Ross and Pauline. She was to fly her new helicopter home and Ross to fly his, having flown the chopper in the week before for a service in readiness for the approaching muster season.

David, and Jane holding Ross Jnr, also waved a fond farewell. Jane was taking the youngster back to the station in the Winnebago and David would follow.

Sophie and Bill were to retire also, he knowing she wanted to spend more time with her friend Pauline on the station. Bill had to admit helping David would be far less stressful than General Practice, things had changed. Red tape and paper work consumed him now and Sophie was not the world's greatest paper shuffler, she was a real people person but hated paperwork. Bill did not want to employ anyone so had sold his practice and it would only be a couple of weeks before it was all over.

Now all standing together they waved as the two helicopters rose in tandem into the blue sky.

"Well folks," David said shielding his eyes, watching both disappear as they became specks on the horizon, "they are going home to what they both love. How lucky are they? Amazing really, just goes to show what people can achieve if they grasp the opportunity."

"Well Bill, see you and Sophie at the station in three

weeks, travel safely" David said, getting into his vehicle, ready to pull in behind Jane.

Pauline relished her new found freedom, completely happy with her achievements. Now she felt she was a complete partner. Both would share all the duties, a complete couple even sharing the exhilaration and danger of mustering.

"I am going to circle Mount Pauline on the way" she informed Ross on her right keeping a close eye on her.

"I might mount Pauline when we get home too" he laughed in reply.

"Okay you two," a voice came over the two way radio "keep the party clean and good luck Pauline, both with the flying and getting mounted!"

They laughed, it was Grant and another pilot also in the air close by on route to the season's first muster.

"Behave you boys, happy mustering. Good luck to you always and many thanks Grant" Pauline replied gazing below her as she streaked over the land she had fallen in love with. Smiling she waved to her husband who waved back. Pauline now felt on an equal footing. Her life was complete, she had endured the cattle yards and now she was a Muster Pilot.

Chapter Seventeen

Nearing the station helipad Pauline swept north to fly over the mountain range named in her honour as Ross glided in for a landing. Pauline was always in awe of the landscape, somehow it had the effect of making her feel a small part in the greater scheme of things. These ranges, millions of years old, exposed just how short a period mankind had actually lived on the planet and she wondered as she broke off and headed back to the homestead just how long humankind would inhabit the planet or if we would destroy ourselves and in fact the planet with greed. Flying the helicopter Pauline found gave her a far different perspective on her life and the natural surrounds in which she now lived, so far removed from the sterile and unrealistic life she had lived in Canberra.

Margaret and Colin were glad to see them home again and had lunch waiting. During the meal they all caught up with the latest news. Heavy monsoonal rains had lashed the station for several weeks and the lush native grasses had boomed. Sonny and Mona had been joined by Billy before the road had closed and he showed no signs of leaving. Pauline and Ross both felt happy at this turn of events, Billy was a steady and quiet worker and his presence was welcome.

David and Jane along with young Ross Jnr turned up just on dusk, the road had still been a bit muddy in patches and caution was needed. The station had been transformed into a family affair with all living in harmony instead of that of a single Ross living alone for months at a time.   David, Sonny and Billy fenced off several paddocks and started cultivating them. The irrigation equipment purchased in Broome would be delivered the following week in readiness for the first of the crops to be sown in David's grand plan. It had been agreed Pauline and Ross would handle the livestock side of the operation along with mustering nearby stations to supplement the station income damaged by the loss of market in Indonesia because of the ban on live exports implemented hastily by the government the previous season to appease the rising influence of the radical environmental movement.

Pauline, now far from the comfort of the halls of power, better understood how the ill-conceived, hastily made decisions in Canberra, by political parties to hold onto power through alliances with the minor parties, had such devastating effects on peoples' lives. Pauline had never considered when in Canberra herself that such decisions could cause so much havoc in the lives of hard working, taxpaying Australians with no option but to simply accept the politics of the day.

On many occasions chatting with her mother, Pauline grasped as did Jane that their past life was in a world so foreign to the one they now lived in, it was inconceivable to even compare the two. No decision they made in their past lives ever had any real impact on them financially or otherwise. Money was simply guaranteed by the taxpayer, its distribution and waste meant nothing to them but now the ramifications of bad decisions and wasteful spending had a direct impact on them. Bankruptcy and the loss of one's property was the result of a bad decision or regulations and laws imposed on them by bureaucrats simply to appease a minority and stay in power.

Sophie and Bill arrived a week later with the news that Sophie was again pregnant and the upcoming event was celebrated that evening over dinner. Sophie admitted to Pauline it had come as a surprise having assumed she was no longer capable of falling pregnant but was happy at the thought of another child. Bill was happy for them to spend the dry season with Pauline and Ross. He knew the old friends delighted in each other's company and Bill very much enjoyed his long standing friendship with David. The old friends drove around the station organising the sorghum crops while Jane and Sophie minded the children. Pauline and Ross worked long hours mustering, both sought after for their skills rounding up cattle on the vast expanses of the Kimberleys.

The families planned to educate the children in Broome when they started their education. Jane and Sophie would look after them during the week while Pauline and Ross along with Bill and David stayed on the station during the dry season. In the wet season it was agreed that all the family would live in Broome until the children had completed their education.

Sophie gave birth to a son they named Ayden, and Bill was ever so proud to have a son even if he had sired him at a late age.

On one of Pauline's rare trips into Fitzroy Crossing with Mona they visited Mona's daughter who had problems with alcohol. Pauline, seeing Mona shocked and distressed at the condition of her daughter's three year old child Mary, decided to take her with them and so arrived home with a foster daughter to rear. The beautiful child, always smiling, became an integral part of the Anderson household and a playmate for Ross Jnr.

Two years passed and Ross Jnr and Mary bid farewell to Pauline and the station, the time had come for them to start school in Broome. Pauline considered this later as perhaps the most heart breaking scene she had witnessed, the big sad eyes of Mary and Ross's tearful wave.

After the freedom of running and playing on the station and mingling with other children the restrictions of school life were foreign to Ross Jnr and Mary and it was here the bond between them both grew, supporting each other during this time of upheaval for them and throughout their learning.

Pauline and Sophie accepted this as part of raising their children, an education was paramount in a changing world and both had a determination to offer their offspring the best available. Pauline now viewed Mary as a part of her family and she planned to educate Ross Jnr and Mary to the best of her ability.

Each evening Pauline would phone and talk to both children who in time settled happily into school life, spending weekends on the station. Either Ross or Pauline would fly in and pick them up returning them of a Sunday. This practice in time ceased when they both began to play sport of a weekend and formed new friendships as they grew older.

187

It was on such an excursion into Broome during the wet season and as an electrical storm approached that David hitched a ride into Broome with Ross. Ross decided to skirt the storm but unfortunately it turned out to be a super storm and engulfed the little helicopter. Even after years of flying Ross had become disorientated when his instrument panel went haywire. Investigations followed but failed to deliver an exact cause of the crash.

Pauline knew Ross, he was an experienced pilot and years later she held fervently to the belief that mechanical error would have been the one and only reason for the accident that claimed her husband and father-in-law, him also the husband of her grieving mother.

Pauline had spent the afternoon helping Sonny and Colin repair a cattle crush in the workshop, watching as Ross and David disappeared into the dark clouds forming to the west she knew, as many times before, to skirt the storm or land if enveloped in inclement weather. It was only after they had been gone several hours that she became alarmed and when told they had not arrived, immediately reported the overdue flight to the authorities who arranged to mount an air search at daylight weather permitting although, usually during the wet, most storms occurred in late afternoon.

She sat in the office and phoned Sophie and her mother Jane in Broome. Pauline knew something terrible had happened but hung on to the hope that they somehow had put the helicopter down safely. Margaret and Colin sat with her all that long night, several times the phone rang the incident having now travelled over the outback like a wildfire and dozens of stations and muster pilots asked if Pauline knew the flight path as they were all waiting to launch a search come daylight.

Several times a distraught Jane phoned her daughter, the thought of them both losing their men was inconceivable. Bill gave Jane a strong sedative to calm her down and often spoke to Pauline. He knew by her behaviour that if the worst happened he would need to get to her fast. Ross had been her one great love, she lived in his shadow. Bill was grateful at least that her son slept soundly in his bed as did young Mary, oblivious of the calamity happening around them.

At 4am Bill phoned the company manager ordering a plane to be on standby at daylight to transport them all to the station, he knew Pauline would not leave it but wait for news there in the home she had made with Ross. Waking the sleeping children including his own, they all sat in the aircraft as the first shards of daylight appeared. The helicopter personally flown by the manager took off and they observed several helicopters already in the air sweeping over the search area. As they circled to land at the station they saw Sonny waiting at the strip ready to pick them up. Usually full of information and jokes, Sonny today was silent.

No one spoke on the way to the homestead, only a short drive away. As they approached Pauline was seated on the edge of the veranda with her head held between her hands and when she looked up at the approaching vehicle Bill knew the worst had happened.

Pulling up, Sonny who had been silent till then released

the cry of his Aboriginal forbears. He knew the family had lost two members, Jane also now knew the worst had happened as she fell into the arms of her daughter both in total shock and disbelief. Sophie stood with the bewildered children, tears streaming down her eyes, the unimaginable had happened.

Both Pauline and Jane lapsed into a state of grief. Their dreams had ended after only a few short years. Sophie and Bill with the help of a distraught Margaret looked after the children, bewildered when told that Ross Snr and their doting grandfather David would never return. A huge crowd attended the funeral as the two men were laid to rest under the African flame tree, in the very spot Pauline and Ross had been married, overlooking the station they both loved so much.

That evening Pauline lay in bed unable to sleep thinking only of her short marriage and the happiness she'd had with Ross, her mind wandering as she pictured them both working together, many times with no conversation passing between them, content in the presence of each other. Now she wished she had told him more often of the love she had for him, that he was her very life. Then hearing something, she turned and her heart melted. Climbing onto the bed were her son, the offspring of her husband, now Ross in his own right, and Mary, neither speaking. Her son needing assurance, cuddled up to her as young Mary also lovingly snuggled into her, seeking comfort.

Somehow for the first time since the accident Pauline drifted off to sleep wedged between the two little children she loved so much. She held them both to her bosom and in that instant knew what she must do, the course she would take. This was the catalyst Pauline needed to take leadership of her fractured and confused family.

The following morning Margaret came in alarmed and seeking the two children but a warm smile crossed her face at the scene before her. Pauline woke and immediately helped dress the children then showering and dressing herself she entered the kitchen. Her mother looking dishevelled and confused sat sipping a coffee. Sophie entered next and sat at the kitchen bench looking at both without speaking.

"Okay Mum and Sophie, I am as shattered at what happened as anyone but last night I decided I must press on. I have a son and another child I class as my daughter to think of and I want to keep the station for Ross. It is his heritage and I intend to run it until he decides to take it over or not. At least he will be given that choice, I am sure his father and indeed his grandfather would have both wished that" Pauline informed them.

"Are you serious Pauline? The ramifications of a woman trying to run this juggernaut are mind-blowing. I suggest you sell and move to a town, educate the children and lead a more sedate life, this is bad enough with a husband but, on your own, get real!" Jane shot back sobbing.

"Mum, my course is set, leave if you wish and live in Broome. Me, here I stay. I can and will run my son's station for him to the best of my ability. Anything else is not an option" Pauline replied.

"Well, for what it's worth, Bill and I will give you all the support we can" Sophie promised.

191

"Okay Pauline life must go on and if that is what you want so be it. I can see your mind is made up" Jane responded in defeat.

"When I married Ross Mum it was for better or worse. I know in my heart he would want me to soldier on as he always did. This was his life, I owe him that" Pauline in a determined voice replied. Margaret listening to the conversation broke in, "Pauline my life is here with you. You can count on Colin and me, just as I am sure you can count on Sonny and Billy working alongside you as long as they can. This is now my home too and to even consider returning to the outside world is frightening."

"Thanks Margaret I will need all the help I can get, we have a few weeks till the wet ends so perhaps we should try to return to normal. A large part of my heart has gone forever but when I look at my son and Mary my course in life is set. I will always mourn what I had and know I can never replace. I intend to honour the man who gave me a new life, one of respect and love. I have done some silly things in my life and intend to spend what time I have left redeeming myself and making Ross proud of me. I know he'll be looking after us wherever he may be!" Pauline replied. All those present knew from here on not to try to divert her from what she was determined to do but to try and return to normal over time. Even though Jane and Sophie both knew the coming years would take a great toll not only on her inner strength and ability but on her mental wellbeing for to fail would be disastrous for Pauline. Her journey from this day forward was going to test the very fibre of her soul.

Chapter Eighteen

The day after her decision Pauline sat in the office charting her future and that of the station. She had stood a wedding photo of her and Ross prominently on the desk and whenever in doubt she looked at it, somehow gaining an inner strength.

In reality she was well aware the destiny of the station lay in her hands, every future decision was hers, any ramifications rested entirely on her shoulders. To try and pass the buck or blame as in her past life as a public servant was never going to be an option. Here in the real world the reality of any given situation was far removed from the spin and unreality of Canberra.

For several hours she thought deeply about every aspect of her situation, deciding to abandon the cropping started by David and to sell the irrigation equipment, the cost and staffing now making it at this time unviable. It had always been a dream of David's to at least try such an enterprise and it had been he who had financed it not really envisaging a profit but simply to keep him occupied. Pauline knew her mother had been left the house in Broome and along with her own savings enough money to keep her comfortable. Pauline wondered though how to keep her busy and to stop her slipping into depression, David had been her one and only real love treating her as an equal and they had shared such wonderful times together. Pauline knew deep down to dwell on the past was in reality wasting one's life and that life went on but to even think of having another relationship was abhorrent, she'd had the best, nothing else was ever to be considered. She remembered a comment Sophie made years ago, that to have a few years of bliss with someone who really loved her and took care of her would be better than nothing and now fully appreciated her friend's thoughts at that time.

That evening Pauline walked to the cattle yards and sitting on the top rail as the sun set a smile came over her face for the first time since the tragedy. She smelled the cattle, heard their bellowing, saw the billowing dust and imagined a younger Pauline dressed ready to seduce Ross but instead falling ungraciously in the dust and cow crap. On reflection she would have done it a thousand times over to have had the few glorious years she'd spent with Ross.

From a distance Sonny stood looking at the small lonely figure, Pauline was his friend and he unconditionally loved her for what she was, tough and resilient. He knew he would never leave the station while ever she lived here and as he turned to go back to his beloved garden his eyes misted. His heart felt for her, he knew Ross had really loved her and having watched them together was aware of the strong bond that existed between them and always would, only the death of Pauline would break it.

The dry soon arrived and to a certain extent normality returned to the station. Pauline spent hours weaving over the landscape rounding up cattle aided by Sonny, Billy and Colin who because of years of experience managed the ground work. Then came days of drafting, branding and loading cattle, a never ending program of long hours, in extremely dusty and trying conditions, all without complaint or dissent. To a man they all respected Pauline and admired her for her grit, determination and dedication.

Jane returned to Broome and along with Sophie cared for the children and monitored their schooling. Still every night Pauline spoke to her son and Mary, sharing each other's news on how both households had spent their day.

Time and the seasons passed by ever so fast as the shy public servant continued her incredible journey. Pauline was admired by all for her uncomplaining and determined spirit. Her flying became legendary, revered by the best.

Mary on reaching the age of sixteen expressed a desire to return to the station and work with Pauline. Her enthusiasm and willingness soon won the respect of Sonny and Billy and Pauline was grateful for her assistance. A strong bond, closer than that of mother and daughter had developed between the two and they became inseparable.

Ross decided to attend university in Perth and Sophie's daughter Rachael followed. Pauline and Sophie at first were worried but both reported they had settled in well and rang home several times weekly. Things settled into a routine. Ross always travelled home for breaks and he and Mary went off hunting and fishing just as they had done in their childhood.

Many times when Sophie visited, the two would sit under the Flame tree and talk about their lives. One day the conversation turned to their lives before coming to the Kimberleys, "You know Sophie" Pauline said turning to her friend, "if you'd told me in Canberra all those years ago that we would be sitting here together in this isolation and beauty discussing our lives I would have considered it preposterous".

"One never knows Pauline" Sophie scoffed "to be honest when I first met you I would have never guessed just what you were capable of when given the chance."

'Ha" Pauline laughed "we have done a few things on reflection that I am not too proud of but 'he who is without sin cast the first stone' I say."

"Pauline, really it was like we had broken free from an old life, we did go a bit silly but we soon became respectable married women and you know my dear Bill has never in all the years we have been married mentioned our behaviour back then" Sophie informed her.

"We both had a bit of luck with our men Sophie and I will never forget Ross to the day I die. He truly loved me so I owe him to keep his station going as long as I can. I hope Ross will come home one day and take over but I will never leave. My happiest times were here with Ross, he treated me as his equal, he nurtured me and let me fly free even now when I am flying I feel him up there with me, watching over me and waving with his silly big smile. It is a feeling even now I cannot explain" Pauline replied.

"Hard to believe the old swearing Pauline has matured so much, like me too I suppose. Do you ever think of one day having a new relationship?" Sophie asked.

"Hell no Sophie, an old weather beaten woman with saggy tits, never even give it a thought. Ross will do me I was lucky. To be honest the bugger made up for lost time and shagged me almost daily so really, in a way, we both made up for lost time" Pauline laughed.

"Pauline we have been friends for a long time so please understand I am not trying to cause problems but Rachael tells me Ross is getting around with a bad mob in Perth. She believes he is trying drugs and even his girlfriend is a wild one" Sophie looking serious told Pauline.

"Sophie thanks, I have been a bit worried he doesn't phone me as much and seems defensive when I ask him questions. He seems always in need of money too. I feel it partly my fault, by isolating him for so long he was unprepared for the real world, it can be a harsh place" Pauline replied and, suddenly concerned, a shudder went down her spine. She had dismissed such thoughts from her mind but now reality hit.

"Perhaps we are both worrying too much, after all he is a sensible young man. Strangely enough I always thought he and Mary would become an item one day" Sophie replied.

"Really! They had always been childhood friends and playmates but I never thought it would go further than that" Pauline replied.

"Oh shit Pauline come on, poor Mary works here month after month waiting for him to come home, watch her big beautiful eyes light up in his presence, she adores him" Sophie explained.

"I must be stupid Sophie, poor Mary I know what it is like to really want someone, what can I do?" Pauline queried, shocked at her stupidity.

"Nothing old friend, even Rachael sees what's going on, you can do nothing but support them both as you always have. Anyhow Margaret has some fish cooked for lunch thanks to Sonny" Sophie replied getting up holding her hand out to her friend and pulling her up from the chair.

Pauline was deep in thought as her mind swirled. The last thing she needed was Ross becoming a drug addict, she knew it was up to her to either take action or wait to see what transpired.

That evening in the office she tried to phone his flat several times. It was unlike him in the past to be out week nights. Pauline had not met his girlfriend and she refused to come home with him on his last trip.

Although at the time she thought nothing of it, she now fathomed the signs had been slowly building, that her son's behaviour was changing and alarm bells now began to ring.

That evening as she lay in bed unable to sleep she decided to head for the kitchen to make a dink. To her surprise Mary was seated at the table drinking coffee.

"Are you okay Mary?" Pauline asked concerned.

"I have been trying to phone Ross but he won't answer" Mary sobbed.

Pauline pulled out a chair and sat down next to Mary. Her heart ached for her and placing an arm around her said, "Perhaps he is busy studying, I know sometimes men can be so thoughtless. Tell you what, go to bed and rest. Next weekend how about you and I fly down to Perth to see him and let's go shopping too, we'll have a wonderful time."

"Really can we do that?" Mary asked happily.

"Of course we can my darling girl, about time we had

a good break I even thought we could do with a new ute so let's buy one and drive it home. It will do us both good and we can make a bit of a holiday of it" Pauline informed her, the news seeming to please Mary.

The following morning after a restless night Pauline as usual with anything to do with Mary walked down to Sonny and Mona's cottage to discuss the coming trip with them. Pauline found Sonny seated, legs crossed, by a small fire watching a billy atop the embers warming up for the first of his many cups of tea for the day.

"Hi Sonny, is Mona still in bed?" Pauline asked.

"Nah she bin cookem up some toast eh" Sonny cheerfully replied as Mona came out of the cottage carrying a plate of toast.

"I came down to tell you that Mary and I are going to Perth for a few days if that is okay with you" Pauline informed them.

"No problem missus you look after her eh" Sonny replied.

"To be honest Sonny I think Ross may have a few problems, I hope to bring him home but will see what happens" Pauline informed her old friend.

"You bringum back eh him belonga here that bad place no good younga fella missus boss" Sonny looking worried told Pauline.

"I'm afraid you are right as usual Sonny but if he refuses then sadly there's not much I can do" Pauline replied.

"You tellum Sonny say come alonga home to his father country him belonga here" Sonny told Pauline.

"I will do my best Sonny, take care of Mona and I will

199

bring back a new ute if I can, you take my old one it is yours now" Pauline told Sonny as she bade them farewell.

Pauline packed with Margaret's help while Mary visited her grandparents. Pauline imagined the instructions being given to her by Sonny as to the pitfalls of 'them big fella cities'.

Pauline knew the station was in safe hands as she drove out the station road to the highway for the long drive to Broome. They would stay with Jane that night and catch the early flight to Perth the following morning. Having fuelled in Fitzroy Crossing, Pauline let Mary drive the rest of the trip as she had a slight headache, caused no doubt by stress as she had been unable to focus on anything else but what she may discover in Perth.

Mary was a competent driver and Pauline dozed fitfully on the trip. Despite all her problems she realised, as she looked at the beautiful childlike face of Mary, just how lucky her life had really been since leaving Canberra all those years ago. She reflected on the love she had shared with Ross and now on what a wonderful family she had both back at the station and in Broome. 'No matter what happens' she thought 'life will endure and I just have to gather the strength to go on. Whatever my son has done or strayed into I must have the strength to guide him back to his destiny.'

Pauline knew she needed to be strong for Mary because she saw no bad in anyone. Vulnerable and trusting of all humanity Mary was one of nature's most beautiful products. She recalled the night Mary and Ross had come into her bed at one of her lowest moments, lifting her from absolute devastation. It was then she had made the decision to keep the station and go on with her life for the sake of the two innocent but troubled children who sought her love and support that terrible night. Pulling into the drive of her mother's house Jane ran out to meet them, the trio each greeting the other as Sophie and Bill too joined the group and embraced Pauline and Mary.

Although thrilled to see each other all felt an underlying tension because of their concern for the wellbeing of one of their own inner circle. Ross, now far away from family and breaking off the constant contact with them, fuelled a strong suspicion that all was not well.

Bill during the evening meal as they exchanged gossip raised the idea of him accompanying Pauline and Mary but Pauline declined his kind offer. In her opinion she was the one who had to rectify the problem and take full responsibility for the mistakes. Sophie implored her not to even think such a thing insisting she had been a perfect mother and that eventually we are all responsible for our own behaviour.

Once again Pauline tried unsuccessfully to phone Ross, increasing her concern. Although they stayed up late talking and she felt exhausted she still found sleep intermittent, constantly waking in fear, her mind starting to wander to all sorts of bad scenarios. Each time however she had the strength to pull herself together knowing it was she who would eventually have to try and fix it, whatever the problem.

Landing at Perth airport mid-morning Pauline and Mary collected their baggage and hired a car. After leaving the airport they pulled up outside the flat Ross rented not far from the university. Pauline was shocked when a girl answered the door and even more so when she said she had never heard of Ross.

Pauline then drove to the University. Here she was informed Ross had not attended classes for several weeks, in fact he had informed them he was taking time out from studies and they assumed he had gone home.

Now really concerned Pauline went straight to the Police Headquarters and informed the desk Sergeant of her concern. Taking details he returned after a short time with a Detective who invited Pauline and Mary into his office.

Pauline sat stunned as she was informed Ross and a girl he was getting around with had been caught bringing drugs in from Bali. Both at this time were in prison awaiting trial. Ross was over eighteen and they had not tried to locate his family as he had refused to give them any details. The Detective on gleaning his personal details was as shocked as Pauline and being a family man himself advised her to hire a lawyer and apply for bail. He was sure it would be granted as long as he resided with his mother. He also informed Pauline that Ross's partner had been suspected for some time of dealing in drugs and he was sure Ross had financed the trip.

Pauline was shocked, unaware Ross had a passport. He must have obtained one without her knowledge.

The Detective seeing their distress gave Pauline the phone number of a Solicitor and told her how to visit her son. Immediately she phoned the Solicitor recommended by the helpful Detective and made an appointment for that afternoon then drove straight to the prison remand centre. She broke down in tears as her son was escorted to the visiting room, he looked absolutely shocking.

When he saw the distress of Mary and his mother Ross broke down sobbing, repeating over and over, "Sorry, Mum and Mary I have let you down badly, I cannot believe what I have done."

Pauline spoke first, "What is done is done, no one is perfect. I have arranged to see a Solicitor. We will get you bailed out and take you home until the court case" Pauline told her son.

"No Mum, I must stand alone on this. You always told me we are responsible for our own destiny, go home and forget me" Ross replied apologetically.

"Ross you will do as our Mum says, no way are we leaving you here" the usually quiet Mary scolded.

Ross, who had avoided eye contact with her, now looked into Mary's big troubled eyes with tears streaming down them. "If you say so Mary how could I ever say no to the best friend I have in the world?" he responded.

"Okay, we are out of time I will go and arrange a Bail Hearing, the Police will not oppose it if you come home with us" Pauline composing herself stood up ready to leave.

"Thanks Mum and Mary I was too proud to let you know, I hoped to get this over with and not let you find out, it was silly of me I suppose" Ross replied.

"Be assured Ross we all at some time in our lives make mistakes but if we admit them and face up to them we can be better people for it, life is a big learning curve."

Pauline now having gained her composure told her son, who looked at them both, thankful he had such a wonderful family.

Chapter Nineteen

On the way to visit the firm of Solicitors Pauline decided with Mary not to inform those waiting in Broome for news. Instead they would just inform them at this stage to save any anxiety that they would all be coming home soon and everything would be explained then. Pauline also stopped at the Toyota dealership and ordered a new Landcruiser Ute arranging to pick it up the next day. They would return the hire car at the same time.

The meeting with the Solicitor was brief. The firm would apply for bail as soon as possible and one of the Court staff would apply the same day for a hearing and visit Ross to be briefed on the matter.

Pauline now felt somewhat relieved although she partly blamed herself. Ross had led a sheltered life not really skilled in the real world and its dangers. She was also relieved by the news from the Detective that the offence would be heard in the lower Court because of the smaller amount involved.

Pauline collected her new ute and Mary followed her in it as they dropped off the hire car. The duo then again visited Ross who was much more talkative. Pauline did remind him of the serious nature of the offence but followed by stating she hoped he had learned a good lesson. She suggested perhaps a year off from University and he agreed. Secretly Pauline hoped he would settle on the station. Her thoughts dwelt on Ross taking over the station as did those of his late father and no University would give him the knowledge to do that, he would learn as she did from the school of hard knocks.

The day of the Hearing arrived and Pauline and Mary sat at the back of the Court and stood as the Magistrate entered. Luckily Ross had his Bail Application heard first, the Solicitor advising the Magistrate that they sought to have Ross released into his mother's care and that she was present in Court. He advised further that his instructions were that a Plea of Guilty be entered and the Defendant wished to have the matter dealt with as soon as possible.

The Police Prosecutor informed the Court he had no issue with the Defendant being released into his mother's care as she ran a well-known and large pastoral station in the Kimberleys. This he advised was Ross's first offence and, although importation of any drug was serious, he informed the Magistrate the amount in question was considered to be at the lower end of the scale.

Ross was given Bail on a surety of ten thousand dollars to be guaranteed by Pauline and as part of the Bail restrictions he was to reside on the station although because of its isolation he was excused from reporting to Police. A hearing date for Plea and Sentence was set down for two months hence and Pauline welcomed her son into her arms as the three left the Court thrilled that, at least for now, they had been reunited.

Pauline found that although she had set up a bank account for Ross it was empty, so gathering his few possessions the trio left Perth and by midday day they were heading north. Pauline still decided that they would take their time and have a few days' break on the way home. They stopped at the shopping centre in Geraldton late in the afternoon and Pauline shouted both Mary and Ross some new clothing, even rewarded Mary with some nice jewellery for her help in convincing Ross to be realistic and come home with them.

Overnighting in a motel they set off early, heading north. Pauline wanted to spend a couple of days and visit Ningaloo Reef so, booking ahead, they drove the entire day arriving that evening. Mary and Ross had driven in turns letting Pauline enjoy the scenery. Although she accepted the seriousness of what Ross had done she felt happy the trio were back together again and the following day they snorkled the reef.

'Perhaps,' Pauline pondered as she watched Mary and Ross, again bonding as when childhood playmates, splashing in the warm water and snorkelling over the reef together 'the simple things and times in one's life are always the best'.

The previous evening Margaret informed her, the Post Contractor who had signed on their behalf for decades had been instructed to no longer deliver registered mail. The reason for the decision, clouded in bullshit. 'Another service stuffed by incompetents, making life harder' Pauline thought, 'now a day's drive to pick up a bloody parcel!'

Mary sat on the beach sorting her few shells as Ross came and sat with his mother, "I am really sorry for what happened Mum, please don't blame anyone, it was my own fault. To be honest I got carried away with Helen, she introduced me to the wildest sex and I became hooked along with the various drugs. Actually I got on a roller coaster and although I knew it was wrong, I didn't want to get off it."

"Listen Ross, even I have my secrets and am a bit ashamed of some of the things I've done but, as long as we realise and accept that, we can change our ways. Sitting here I've been wondering if perhaps I am pushing you and Mary into a life neither of you want. I suppose you know Mary worships the ground you walk on, so one thing I ask of you, or even beg of you, please never hurt her. She is a child of nature. I've just been thinking that the simple things in life are always best and look how happy she is just picking up a few shells. I want you tell me if you do not want to take on the station. Just because it was your father's life doesn't mean it has to be yours and times are changing fast. On reflection I suppose I became a little too focused on working all these years to keep your heritage going and of late I've often wondered if I did the right thing."

"I look at the world around me Mum and honestly my best memories are on the station, somehow it seems like a refuge and separate from the real world. I make no promises, but perhaps I will have a year at home after the court case and serving my sentence whatever it may be, then we will sit down and decide. I worry about you Mum and feel ashamed for not thinking of you and Mary. It was selfish of me and I owe you both an apology" Ross solemnly replied.

"I have not mentioned this before but what about this Helen you speak of, is she okay? If you have responsibilities you must face them" Pauline questioned her son.

"No not really, she actually turned on me at the airport when they found the drugs and told the officials I was the culprit, that it was my idea and that I financed it. I'm not trying to pass the buck in anyway, but truthfully I went along with it and accepted the blame although she planned the whole trip and had already done several trips for him before, so knew the dealer well. Like I said, it was the sex and drugs, along with the wild party scene I was trapped in, not Helen. She used me but when all the money I gave her began running out she lost interest. Anyway, it's over" Ross replied.

"Thanks for being honest, I'll not mention it again but when we get home please tell your grandmother Jane as well as Uncle Bill and Auntie Sophie the truth, just as you told me. We have never had secrets, they are family" Pauline requested.

Mary came along and sat beside Pauline who placed her arms around them both, "You two are my very favourite people in the whole world" she told them "I am sorry if sometimes I seem bossy but I do try to do what is best for us all."

"Mum I love you, you have never ever been nasty to either of us, and Ross knows that just as well as I do!" Mary cuddled Pauline as a tear trickled down her cheek.

"You know guys I have learnt many a lesson in my life and I want you to learn from those and my mistakes as well. I'm sorry your father and Grandfather Ross died, they were two special people and you would have learnt so much from them too. You are the lights of my life and my love for you both is unconditional. I think sometimes we fail by not telling those close to us just how we feel about them and sometimes leave it too late. One thing is for sure, we can never go back. We have no rush to get home let's spend an extra day here just sitting on the beach and relaxing. Life speeds by so fast" Pauline told them.

"Come on then Mary, grab Mum and let's go for a long walk, I will find you a nice clam shell each to take home for a soap holder" Ross promised as he dragged them both to their feet.

Pauline followed the pair along the beach for a couple of hours, watching them enjoy the freedom and tranquility of the area and for the first time in several years, she felt truly relaxed.

Reflecting on her somewhat chaotic life Pauline was grateful to her mother and to Sophie for the chance she was given by circumstance many years before. Never in her wildest dreams would she have thought herself capable of achieving what she had but now believed most people if given the same chance may surprise themselves if faced with similar, almost insurmountable problems. 'The human spirit', she thought, 'was amazing'.

Even Pauline, pleasantly surprised at how relaxed she had become, felt sorry when they packed the Landcruiser and proceeded north to Broome, eventually pulling into the drive two days later to a happy reunion.

Over a barbecue in Bill and Sophie's pool area, Ross shocked them and Jane by telling them of his pending court case and how he had been detected carrying drugs into Perth airport. Sophie was the first, as usual, to show unconditional support for Ross and to cheer everyone up.

"Well, it was only dope and I suppose I must be honest, in my young days, I smoked enough of it. Perhaps we have all done something to be ashamed of in our past. What happened has happened and Ross is honest enough to admit it and to face the consequences, so let's not be too judgemental" Sophie told them all in her usual forthright manner, adding "so, no matter what Ross, if I can do anything at all, you only have to ask".

"I support what my wife says one hundred percent" Bill said rising to his feet.

"Me too Ross, I can tell you, your late Grandfather on your Mum's side was an absolute dead shit. At least you are honest enough to admit a mistake or wrongdoing and I am proud of you" Jane told him as she hugged her grandson.

Rachael and Mary both hugged Ross. He felt relieved that was over but he still had to face the family on the station and was positive old Sonny and Colin would scold him severely and not be so forgiving. In fact Sonny often complained the old tribal ways had disappeared and white man's law forbade the 'old spear in the leg trick' to keep younger members from breaking traditional laws.

When they did arrive back at the station they were warmly greeted by all. Ross with some trepidation, at Mary's and Pauline's goading and before even unpacking their cases, decided to inform the others over coffee of the circumstances. No one spoke although old Margaret walked over and gave him a hug and Colin patted him on the back but old Sonny after a few minutes of reflection pointed a finger at Ross and told him "You belonga here in your family country, not in that big city place with all them bad fella. Getum big problem now you see. Your father good fella, you not go that bad place again eh."

Sonny and Billy walked off with old Mona silently following. Ross knew as did Pauline that for him to regain Sonny's respect would take some time. He had a strong sense of justice in his strange way and forgiveness had to be earned, not given freely.

Pauline was glad to be home, she had always felt comfortable here working long hours and separate from the outside world in many ways. Regardless of the punishment still awaiting Ross, she had enjoyed the trip because it had given her time to reflect and to be alone with Mary and Ross, delighting in their company without the distraction of others.

Pauline decided to commence mustering immediately, although weeks earlier than usual. She recognised the need to return to normality as soon as possible and wanted also to finish prior to the pending court proceedings in case for whatever reason she may have to be absent for some time. If Ross were to receive a custodial sentence she had decided to stay in close proximity of his incarceration for the duration. Although she had not discussed this option she was determined to support her son whatever the outcome.

Pauline soon identified Ross had some problems settling back into station life after two years in Perth although he did not complain, and worked side by side with Sonny and the crew in the yards. Often he appeared distant and it was only Mary who seemed able to cheer him up, realising also perhaps that the strain of the forthcoming court case was impacting on him as it drew ever closer.

Because of the unsafe state of the station roads so soon after the wet season, it was decided to hold the saleable cattle in the previously cropping paddocks, well fenced and full of feed. Colin and Sonny would yard and load later while Pauline was in Perth or when road conditions improved. Mary, much to Sonny's anguish, had also expressed her desire to go with Pauline and Ross to Perth for the hearing.

Too soon the day had arrived when Pauline, Mary and Ross waved a sad farewell to the station crew who wished them all the best with many hugs and kisses. Even Pauline normally always positive, felt a sense of apprehension as they drove towards Broome to stay overnight with Jane before flying to Perth.

The trio sat nervously waiting for the Magistrate to enter the court room. Luckily, Pauline noticed, apart from their Solicitor and the Prosecutor, no one else was present.

When the Magistrate entered, the security officer came into the court and ushered Ross to the stand. The Prosecutor read the charges and the Magistrate asked for a Plea. Ross stated clearly "guilty".

Their Solicitor detailed the Defendant's background and that of his family. Of his mother who sat in court and her long battle alone to keep the family station going. Of his apology to the court for the crime he had openly admitted and which was his client's first offence.

When he had finished Pauline felt sick. She had just

recognised the Magistrate as being the one who handled the Bail Application and he was about to pass sentence.

"I am sure young man you come from a good family. However the offence is a serious one and drugs are becoming a scourge on today's society. I therefore sentence you to six months' gaol, wholly suspended, on the condition that you be put on a Good Behaviour Bond of two years. If you reoffend during that time, let me make it clear, you will serve the sentence in full plus any further the court may issue. You are now free to go. The Clerk will have the necessary papers ready to sign within the next hour."

At first Pauline and Mary heard the sentence of six months and collapsed in the court. It was only when the Magistrate finished and their Solicitor and Ross approached smiling, that they both knew Ross was not going to gaol.

The Solicitor ushered them from the court into the waiting room. No one spoke but all held hands tightly, it had been a traumatic time. Mary phoned Broome and the station, all were relieved Ross was coming home. The drama had ended better than most expected and signing the documents Pauline suggested heading back to the hotel. She felt quite ill, the stress having finally caught up with her. Ross and Mary agreed. They too did not feel like doing much but just relax, catch up on some sleep and get ready for the flight home when they booked one.

Chapter Twenty

Pauline suggested a day's rest and perhaps a bit of shopping before returning to Broome the following day. Somehow she felt she needed to relax before the trip home and no doubt the problems of running a large station. For the first time since her marriage she felt somewhat flat. Now in her sixties, time she decided was catching up. If Ross did not show an aptitude or keenness to take over the station she now faced the realisation she would be unable to keep going on as she had done since her husband's death. All her old staff members, and indeed her mother, although still in good health would be unable to continue much longer. Pauline knew too that she had a responsibility not to throw away the years of loyalty and hard work Sonny, Mona, Margaret and Colin had given her and whose friendship helped her through the darkest of days.

That morning they had a good lay in and went into the city for lunch. With the trauma of the court case behind them Pauline noticed Ross and Mary had both relaxed. Shopping that afternoon Ross dutifully carried the parcels as Mary and Pauline purchased new western shirts and jeans. Like all young women Mary enjoyed the shopping, trying on various garments while Pauline and Ross watched on, nodding in agreement at her choices. Since leaving school Mary had, like all the other station workers, been paid wages and although rural staff wages never competed or reached the crazy heights of the mining industry, she had saved under the guidance of Pauline and with free board and meals as part of the package, had built up a nice little nest egg. Pauline however always liked to pay for most of Mary's clothes in appreciation of her efforts and long hours gladly given without complaint.

The following morning waiting at the airport, Ross informed his mother perhaps what she had been hoping for since he had returned to the family fold, "Mum I have given the last few months of my life a lot of thought and decided to stay and help you and Mary on the station. The last couple of years have been a good lesson in life, old Sonny was so right, my life is among those I love and on the station. We live a different life to most city people. We work hard and long hours but it is something difficult to explain, once it traps you, as it did you Mum, nothing else gives the same satisfaction somehow."

"Thanks Ross you have no idea how happy you have made me, when we get back let's book you in for helicopter training, it's time you took over everything. I'll help Mary on the ground" Pauline sobbed as they all hugged.

"Okay Mum but Mary can train too, we could be a team like you and Dad" Ross replied looking at a smiling Mary.

At first Pauline was reluctant but on the way home she reflected on what Ross had said. 'He was right' she thought 'and they would be a good team to run the station. Mary was bright and responsible'. It fitted into the scheme of things perfectly and when they arrived in Broome they immediately started taking lessons.

Pauline decided to stay in Broome with her ageing

mother for a couple of weeks. She really felt like a break with her mother and Sophie, visiting the beach, relaxing and taking coffee breaks at the Boulevard and Chinatown shopping centres.

One afternoon while the trio sat chatting in the Boulevard, Pauline noticed a man sitting opposite on his own, frowning at them. Several times Pauline glanced at Sophie who also saw him frowning at them, as if he recognised them. As they got up to leave he approached, "Sorry I do not wish to intrude but are you Pauline and Sophie? I am Mark, we met many years ago on the road" Mark said.

Sophie spoke first, "Mark of course. Pauline you stay here and catch up on the news, Jane and I have an appointment. We will come back in half an hour or so. Sorry we have to leave Mark, would love to find out what you have been doing."

Pauline nodded in agreement. She had been going to browse the shops while waiting for Sophie and Jane but was inquisitive enough to want to know what had happened to Mark since their meeting all those years ago, and why he was in Broome.

"How did you meet?" Jane broke in as she was leaving.

"Mum you would not want to know" Pauline laughed as they sat back down.

"You first" Pauline smiled as Mark sat down.

"Well Pauline to be honest, often wondered what you two got up to after you left me that night. I was sorry I didn't get your phone number but then I suppose, I was still married. I went onto the mines and for a few years worked in Queensland. My marriage eventually broke up, my wife wouldn't leave Tasmania. Actually she met someone else so perhaps, karma" Mark laughed.

"How come you are in Broome?" Pauline asked

"Well I rose up in the mining ranks and ended up in Karratha as a Supervisor. Got sick of it and retired last week. Sold my house there for a mint while the going was good and here I am in a beat up old camper, roaming free" Mark laughed.

Pauline then filled him in on her story to date, exactly, no holds barred, she trusted him, somehow a blast from the past. When she finished he gave a low whistle.

"Bloody hell Pauline, knew you were some woman but that is amazing. What happened to the Winnebago?" Mark enquired.

"In the shed on the station, still in excellent order, still drive it a bit but rarely these days" Pauline laughed, feeling relaxed. It was good to share her story with someone she'd had a sexual fling with all those years ago.

"Would you consider selling it to me? I was on my way to Darwin to buy something bigger" Mark asked.

"Well, I vowed I would keep it forever but on reflection should have sold it years ago. Come with me for a drive tomorrow and let's see what we can work out" Pauline suggested, accepting now that realistically it would have to be sold one day.

"Great," Mark replied "I'll drive out with you when you leave."

"If you like, fly out with me, then if we strike a deal you can drive it back and sell your old camper here" Pauline offered.

"Fine, I am camped in the Golf Club grounds, what time do you want to leave?" Mark asked.

"Tell you what Mark, follow us home in your van, stay in my Mum's backyard and you can have a meal with us tonight," Pauline invited "then we can both drive out to my helicopter first thing tomorrow. I was heading home anyway."

"Great, cannot believe after all these years coming across you and Sophie again" Mark chuckled, enjoying the company and conversation.

"Bill and Sophie live next door so, perhaps a bit discreet as to how we met" Pauline laughingly cautioned.

"That was in our past Pauline, be assured that is where it will stay" Mark chuckled.

The time seemed to fly by as they talked, filling in the years since they met so long ago. Sophie and Jane returned and seemed happy to have Mark accompany them and to stay for the night.

Bill was more than happy to meet the girls' old friend. Mary and Ross at first seemed a little indifferent towards the intruder but after the meal soon settled when Mark seemed interested in their flying endeavours and shared with them his knowledge of the mining industry.

The following morning Pauline buckled Mark into her helicopter and they rose into the wild blue yonder, Mark praising Pauline for her flying ability as they skimmed across the vast landscape. Chatting about mustering and the various landmarks below, Mark was more than impressed with the knowledge Pauline had accumulated, shaking his head as she described the ranges and river systems as they passed over them.

Landing at the station Mark congratulated Pauline on her flying ability remarking that no one ever really knew what path life would lead them on. Margaret had food waiting on the table as usual for people returning from Broome who it seemed always needed a meal on arrival. Sitting around the table chatting, Margaret raised the question of how they met. Pauline laughed and told her they had in the past enjoyed a good bonk.

After lunch Mark was anxious to look at the old Winnebago and gave a low whistle at its age. Pauline had kept it in perfect condition. Settling on a fair price they shook hands and Mark drove it back to the homestead so Pauline could remove the few clothes still stored in the wardrobe. Pauline invited him to stay a couple of extra days if he wished as flying in he had shown interest in exploring a real working cattle station. Mark accepted the invitation with glee.

Pauline admitted to herself that she relished the company. Mark was easy going and enjoyed a good laugh.

That afternoon Mark accompanied Sonny on one of his fishing expeditions and returned in the evening with fresh barramundi for dinner, excited about the ease with which he had caught several fine fish. Sonny explained that in the 'wet', barra fishing was one of his favourite passtimes, as that was when they were 'on the bite'.

Rising early the following morning, Pauline and Mark set off for one of the far flung regions of the station with a lunch Margaret had packed as usual. On the way Pauline pointed out areas of interest, relaying stories about her experiences over the years and how often she and Ross would land the helicopters at their favourite pools for a skinny dip.

Mark listened intently, happy to hear her fascinating stories. Looking at her he said "Pauline what you have is an incredible story, you are lucky to really have found true love and a soul mate in your late husband, he must have been a special human being. Just one request from an old friend, can you take me to one of the pools for a swim later, it sounds refreshing?"

"You're quite right Mark. Ross was my true love and soul mate and certainly a special human being. Yes, a swim sounds great, have not had one for years to be honest. I have no bathers but then I have nothing you have not seen already" she laughed.

Pauline was having a great time. This was the very first time she had the privilege of showing anyone around her empire, the place that had consumed her for the past twenty five years of her life. She felt safe in Mark's company, like her he had travelled a long and sometimes lonely path in his life. Now all he really wanted to do, he informed her, was relax and travel back to Tasmania to visit his two daughters, now both married with families.

Stopping about 1pm when the sun was at its highest, they enjoyed lunch under the shade of a huge overhang, water cascading down into a small crystal clear pool below. Pauline pointed out the spot she had previously landed in the helicopter, seemingly a lifetime ago and the two old friends chatted for some time. The wet season had not quite ended and the humidity was high so both decided to go for a dip in the inviting water. Undressing to Pauline in front of Mark did not seem strange and taking his hand they walked to the water. Plunging into its refreshing coolness Pauline felt young again, it was so invigorating. Looking at the grassy bank she felt a tinge of sadness, many times she and Ross had become entwined in wild sex sessions after each swim. She almost felt him pick her up and carry her to the bank, taking her passionately, then returning to the water covered in sweat after their prolonged love making.

Pauline enjoyed her dip and returned to the bank, laying on the grass as was her practice, to dry in the warm sun. She was almost dozing when she looked up and Mark was standing above her smiling, still dripping wet, with a huge erection. Without thinking she opened her legs wide raising her knees in expectation as he lay down on her kissing her gently. She gave a small groan as he entered her, at first slowly then unable to control himself he thrust wildly, shuddering as she felt him ejaculate, collapsing on her then rolling off.

Pauline had not envisaged such a happening but now laying there she admitted to herself she had enjoyed the intimacy.

"Sorry Pauline, you looked so inviting, couldn't help myself" Mark apologised.

"To be honest Mark, never thought of us bonking again but I enjoyed it, so don't feel bad" Pauline replied rolling on her side, looking at him laying there like an impish child.

"Tell you one thing old girl, you are still a good bonk"

Mark chuckled.

"Well Mark you may have enjoyed it, but now you have started my lust, let's finish it properly" Pauline replied rolling over on top of him grinding her hips down onto his flaccid penis.

After some time teasing and pleasuring each other Pauline took him in her hand. Rolling her tongue around his swelling cock she rose up slightly and slid down on his throbbing member. Mark grabbed her by the buttocks rising with her, both sweating as they pounded each other. Pauline felt sexual for the first time in a long time and knew her orgasm was approaching, then as small sighs came from her she climaxed, causing Mark to come with her, both collapsing, gasping for air.

"Bloody hell, Pauline that was the best fuck I have ever had" Mark told her still gasping for breath.

"Tell you what Mark, I thought that would never happen again but honestly, I really needed it" Pauline replied.

Resting for some time they again went for a refreshing swim and laying in the sun after, relaxing and drying off, they chatted about life in general, of family and friends. Pauline felt relaxed and happily accepted that her sexuality still existed. Although not in love with Mark, she trusted him and felt comfortable in his presence. For him, like for her the sex had been for sex only, she was sure of that, just good friends pleasuring each other and satisfying pent up sexual needs.

Dressing, they returned to the station and after showering Pauline again spent time in the office, sorry that Mark was going back to Broome the following day to sell his old camper and continue his journey. She had enjoyed their interlude and now understood why her mother, even at her age, had enjoyed intimacy so much. Still sitting in the office later that evening Pauline was actually happy when Mark came in carrying two cups of hot chocolate. "A nightcap for you Pauline and thanks for such a wonderful time, we will always be friends and I will keep in touch" he promised as he sat down opposite.

Pauline looked at him and replied, "Sorry to see you go but I know you have planned to travel on and visit your family. Let's spend our last night together, you've lit my fire again, naughty man!"

Just then the phone rang and after a short conversation Pauline hung up smiling. "That was Grant the instructor, both Mary and Ross are doing well with their flying. Grant is especially happy with Mary. She is steady and a confident student. All in all I have had a good day".

"Great for you Pauline, fingers crossed you'll have a bit of weight lifted from your shoulders at long last. Both are fine young people and you have every right to be proud of them" Mark told her.

Finishing the nightcap Pauline led him to her bedroom. Undressing, they became immediately wrapped in an embrace both enjoying each other's company and the intimacy and sexual gratification they brought to one another.

Pauline woke with a start. The office phone was ringing persistently. Lifting the leg Mark had draped over her, she ran to the office. She knew it would be something urgent for someone to phone at this time. Glancing at the clock on the desk she saw it was 1am and picking up the phone she heard Mary sobbing as she answered.

"Mum, Uncle Bill has passed away in his sleep. Sophie is beside herself, can you come at once?" she pleaded.

"Is Mum and Ross still with her?" Sophie asked.

"Yes, the ambulance is here, they're taking him away right now. Rachael and Ayden are coming home today when they can get a flight from Perth. Mum, she really needs you" Mary implored.

"Okay Mary, tell her I am on my way, if we leave now we can be there by mid-morning. You and Ross stay with her until I get there. Look after Mum too, she is always upset when she loses someone so close" Pauline said gravely.

Hanging up, Pauline raced back to the room. Mark was sitting up in bed, aware that something bad had happened.

"Bill just passed away Mark and I must get to Broome asap! Can you get the Winnebago ready while I dress? If we drive all night we'll hopefully be there mid-morning. If I wait to fly in, it will be mid-afternoon and Sophie needs me."

"Right, no problems" Mark replied bouncing out of bed, pulling on his trousers and shirt.

Pauline dressed and woke Margaret and Colin, telling the shocked pair the sad news. Mark had the Winnebago running by the time she jumped in and immediately drove off into the night. Pauline was ever so grateful he had been with her, such a long drive late at night was a daunting task in any event but even more so had she been alone.

Deciding to stay awake if possible Pauline chatted

with Mark. It was an hour's drive to the highway and, if all went well six more hours to Broome, all the while dodging the wildlife and cattle that frequented the roads at this time of the day.

Pauline knew Sophie would be devastated, she really loved old Bill, he had given her a wonderful life and had been her anchor at a time she really needed it. Pauline often wondered how different their lives would have been if they had not met him on that momentous night all those years ago.

Chapter Twenty-One

Mark drove without stopping, pulling up at Sophie's home at 9.30am, having made the trip in excellent time.

Rushing inside, Pauline found Jane and Ross sitting on the lounge, both looking exhausted. Giving them a hug, she was informed Sophie was in the bedroom. Bursting into the room Pauline collapsed into the arms of her old friend, both unable to hold back their tears.

For some time they lay on the bed entwined in grief, "Sorry Pauline" Sophie sobbed, "I was a bit stupid I suppose, never thinking Bill would die. Ever since we met he was always here for me, such a special person my Bill and now he has gone I know just how you felt when you lost Ross."

"Sophie you once told me that a few years of bliss with someone who really loved you and took care of you would be better than nothing. You had many great years with Bill and two wonderful children" Pauline reminded her as Jane came into the room.

"We have all lost wonderful men now Sophie but at least we had the best. Bill was like David and Ross, three of nature's gentlemen, how lucky were we?" Jane sobbed, wiping her tears.

Pauline saw how frail her mother had become. Since the death of David and Ross her spirit had faded and she'd lost the zest for life David had given her. Bill exposed the real Jane when he met her, vibrant and even swearing, foreign to her mother when living as a family with her late father. Bill had freed her spirit and now she waited in the hope she would somehow join him in the afterlife.

Mary returned from the airport with Sophie's two children, now young adults. Rachael was married and expecting her second child while Ayden was at University studying medicine and planning to follow in his father's footsteps.

Pauline and Jane left them alone with their mother, all three grieving the loss of a wonderful husband and father. Both hugged a red-eyed Mary who had formed a special affection for Bill over the years. He had been her mentor and special friend. She was taking his death very hard and like many never thought of Bill ever dying, he had always been a confidante and elder of the family.

Again Pauline was appreciative of Mark who took upon himself the role of food provider for the grieving family. Quietly behind the scenes, he attended to the meals over the next few days while the funeral arrangements were being made. Bill had requested that he be buried on the station with David and Ross. He explained in a letter to Sophie that he and David had been lifelong friends and he hoped perhaps that she may consider following him later and be buried next to him on the station.

So it was, with dark clouds boiling up in the west, the grieving family laid Bill to rest a week later, alongside his best friend in a quiet ceremony attended only by family members, again Bill's personal wish. Pauline watched, her eyes misting over as the coffin was lowered. Holding her best friend's hand she knew here in this place of raw beauty and isolation Bill would sleep peacefully alongside those on whose lives he had had such a profound effect.

Sophie and Jane both decided to stay with Pauline for a few days after the funeral. Mary and Ross returned to Broome to finish the helicopter course and Sophie's two returned to family and university in Perth. Somehow Mark seemed to blend into the family, staying in the background, thoughtfully helping wherever possible. Pauline became used to him in her bed during this period and he gave her the comfort and intimacy missing from her life.

The next few weeks saw neither Sophie nor Jane wanting to return to Broome. Both now seemed happy to blend into the station life, perhaps because of the close proximity of their respective husbands. Mark never mentioned leaving either although Pauline knew he wanted to visit his children. She had even suggested one night laying in bed that she accompany him after the muster season the following year but Mark just suggested casually that they 'wait and see what happens'. He seemed quite happy going off each day with old Sonny, helping out and gardening.

Mary and Ross arrived home as qualified Muster Pilots and because the station now only had one helicopter they divided the flying, on most occasions one of them acting as a spotter. Although much older, the other participants managed to finish the muster and wave farewell to the last truck load of cattle without any problems. Jane and Mark supplied the food and helped old Sonny, Pauline, Billy and Colin when needed without complaint, often joking that they were the 'pensioner crew'.

Sophie being her resilient self, soon settled into normality showing no signs of wanting to return to her home in Broome. She was a people's person and Pauline knew that to now live on her own was not an option so happily agreed when Sophie asked to join her and Mark, helping out on the station.

Ross and Mary now, with Pauline's guidance, attended to the office work and took over the day to day decision making regarding the station's management.

Much to Pauline's relief, Ross settled into station life. He seemed happy and he and Mary became inseparable. Pauline noticed they had started to share the same bedroom. No one commented, but all seemingly knew that one day the inevitable would happen.

Then, although there was no mention of marriage, Mary started to show signs of pregnancy to everyone's delight, especially Sonny and Mona. Pauline decided to move out of the master bedroom and move Mary and Ross in, it was bigger and had an ensuite. Neither of them said anything when told the decision had been made and indeed when they returned one evening all their belongings had been moved. The final transition to management, in Pauline's eyes, was complete.

The Winnebago still sat in the shed with Mark taking over the care of it, starting it every few days and keeping it clean. Normality seemed to return with the seasons. Mary gave birth to a baby girl they named Elspeth at a simple Christening ceremony under the flame tree. Ross and Mary married at the same time keeping it a surprise to all. Like his father before him Ross did not like large crowds. He never mentioned his time in Perth, simply erasing that episode from his life. He now made his life, as did generations of his family, living in isolation content to spend his days with Mary working with her in partnership as his parents had done, and once again the older women looked after the infant in her parents' absence.

Pauline often sat with Sophie on the porch sharing a coffee break and reminiscing about old times. On one such occasion Pauline mentioned to Sophie Mark's wish to visit his children.

"Why don't we both go Pauline? One last hoorah! Perhaps visit Canberra. We have never been to Tasmania or even to Queensland and if we don't soon go we'll never go" Sophie suggested excitedly.

"Do you mean all three of us?" Pauline asked.

"Of course" Sophie replied "we can share the bed, you can sleep next to Mark. I'm sure at our age no one cares!"

"That wouldn't be a problem to me Sophie, Mark and I shack up because it suits us both. He has had us both before and to be honest if you want to share him it would not faze me. Perhaps for it to work, let him shag us both if he wants to" Pauline chuckled.

"I'm like you Pauline, doesn't faze me one way or the other, but we would need to be open about it with Mark. Really, when you think of it, it would be a bit awkward if we tried to be modest in such close proximity. Let's be natural if we go, and see what happens. Enjoying the trip is the main purpose I suppose" Sophie replied.

That evening in bed Pauline told Mark of their travelling plans. He was thrilled to be going to see his family and even more thrilled to be going with Pauline and Sophie.

The thought of weeks on his own without the comforts he enjoyed with Pauline was not an option. He enjoyed their friendship and intimacy too much. Mark made frenzied love to her that evening and she knew it was the erotic thought of bedding both women again that sexually charged him. On her return from the bathroom and on the spur of the moment she opened Sophie's bedroom door indicating for her to follow.

Sophie was sleeping naked and went to put on a dressing gown. Pauline smiled "You won't need that Sophie, just follow me!"

Sophie knew instantly what Pauline had planned and holding hands they entered the bedroom slipping in either side of Mark who unable to help himself mounted Sophie, thrusting like a wild bull. Several times during the night they copulated, turned on by the erotic sounds each other made, their sexual urges at full throttle. It was erotic and stimulating to watch each other, free to participate in sexual activity for pleasure only. They all knew their shared relationship would work because no expectations existed between them other than that of mutual satisfaction.

That morning even Mark admitted it was stimulating to again have them both in his bed. He remembered always their first encounter, his performance enhanced by the eroticism. Over the years the thought of that encounter often triggered an erection. He admitted surprise though that he could still perform as well, and promised to keep the sexual trysts as interesting and fulfilling as possible.

Once again the Winnebago was parked outside the

homestead as they began their preparations and packing. The family, although at first surprised, warmed to the idea admitting, perhaps of all, Pauline had earned a break. For years she had dedicated her life to the station and now it was her time, even Jane gave her blessing. She would stay with her great grandchild, on the station she now regarded as her home and had no intention of leaving.

With the first signs of the weather heating up and storm clouds gathering, the trio in the Winnebago waved farewell and departed for one last adventure.

The first night they made it to Katherine and, having all been to Darwin decided to stay overnight and head south the following day. After eating a small meal they took a swim in the springs and all three feeling refreshed, climbed into bed.

Although having had a regular sexual relationship for some time, the presence of Sophie in the bed and her appetite for sex inspired Pauline to compete for intimacy. Mark was in his element as he lay between the two women each vying for his attention, both unaware he had gone to a doctor that afternoon for some Viagra. With the girls teasing him he became rock hard and taking turns they sat on him, both satisfying themselves as he seemed to go on forever bringing them to orgasm, then he mounted Pauline and pounded her until he ejaculated.

As morning came he even surprised himself to be pounding Sophie doggy fashion, but knew having both of them turned him on. They too found it erotic to watch each other enjoying the act of sex without constraint, seeking pleasure and trying to outdo each other to satisfy

Mark, who was relishing his luck in again finding them and thankful for the circumstances that delivered both once more into his bed.

As the journey progressed they all became more relaxed, taking it in turns to drive, several times pulling in early to overnight stops, resting and reading, foreign to Pauline who never had the time since arriving in the north for such pursuits. They honed their sexual skills by finding out what turned each other on, completely open as to their wants and feelings. They often experimented trying different positions and acts, the more erotic the better. Their increased demands made Mark stronger, and his lovemaking more prolonged, satisfying them both.

All the news from home was good. Mary was pregnant again but would not deliver until their holiday, planned to last six months, was over.

The trio decided to go via Mount Isa, down the Matilda Highway through Queensland into New South Wales and finally to Canberra. For several weeks they visited country towns and places the girls had heard of but never seen and were happy now they had made the decision to accompany Mark. He was a true friend and good company. Perhaps, Sophie often joked with Pauline, their relationship with him was perfect. For them both, at their age and widowed with no intention of remarrying, their delight in all sharing each other's company on this trip of convenience was exciting and very enjoyable.

Around the campfire one night at St George in Queensland, Pauline reflecting on her life told her companions, "I always feel as though my life has been divided into two parts.

The first was the sterility and unreality of Canberra. The second was private enterprise in its most raw state. No room for mistakes, or bankruptcy resulted and no excuses, or the taxing of workers to pay for your incompetence. Perhaps I am too simplistic but it was far more satisfying for me to run the station. Somehow I felt proud of my achievements and still do. If Ross and Mary make it or don't, is not the point, I held it for them all those hard years, now I must stay back, not interfere. This is our time, some may think us disgusting but life is meant to be lived and my sexuality is important to me. The three of us owe nobody anything. We have made our mistakes and paid our dues. I do have one more wish though, when we finish this trip can we all live in Broome together and, while we're capable, go to the station to help muster? I am no good now on my own and we are three independent friends. Please let us keep the relationship we have, it is perfect as we enter the final period of our lives?"

"Bloody oath Pauline, never heard you say so much in all the years I've known you, but agree with you one hundred percent. We are a perfect team and with you pair around something always seems to be happening. If Mark agrees, let's go for it" Sophie replied.

"You kidding girls, old Mark's in heaven, sometimes I think things are meant to be! Only one thing though, I have my pride when it comes to money and always want to pay my share. What say instead of fighting each time we buy fuel etc. we have a money pool, all putting in so much to meet expenses? Let's keep our relationship on equal terms" Mark remarked.

235

"Mark I am sorry, never thought of that. Yes we are all comfortably well off, so what you suggest is a good idea and I'm sure Sophie would agree" Pauline replied.

"Sophie agrees!" Sophie piped up. "If this is long term let's agree on the rules, our relationship must be satisfactory to us all. One thing, whose place will we live in in Broome? Can we please live in mine, I miss the pool and I am sure Mark would like skinny dipping with two old tarts" she added.

"That would be sensible and Ross and Mary can have Mum's home. She is leaving it to them anyway at my suggestion. So now that is decided, are we all happy?" Pauline asked. By way of confirmation they all stood and raised their glasses to toast the relationship.

She had been aware Mark was uncomfortable with her and Sophie insisting on paying for the costs on the trip but with Mark having paid her for the Winnebago she simply thought she should meet the expenses. She now understood his feelings and was happy they'd sorted everything out.

Arriving in Canberra they actually felt disappointed, it seemed drab and lifeless and had grown immensely. Pauline found it hard to believe how many public servants there were now, spending their days living in a fantasy world so far removed from reality. She was even more aware too just how secretive and shambolic politics had become, all Parties with their share of self-indulgent hypocrites often with huge egos, self-serving and acting in their own best interests.

Pondering over her time spent here she now became

conscious of the futility of it all. Society and business in general, as well as the country, would operate far better if the whole place imploded and along with it all the red tape and the taxing of many out of business purely to fuel the 'I want mentality' of those who believed the country owed them a living without working for it, seemingly unaware or unconcerned that all government funds had to come from the people via taxes directly or indirectly. Governments she knew simply squandered the people's money in order to stay in power. All over the world now citizens marched in the streets as harsh economic sanctions, caused through debt by inept and corrupt politicians, bankrupted once wealthy nations. She wondered how long before the same scenario would take effect here. Pauline knew too that the politicians pandered to the international bankers enslaving the populace to the economic system. Few Australians even knew the Federal Reserve Bank was in fact not owned by Australia but by the banking cartels.

Sophie and Pauline wanted to leave the following day. The place conjured up bad memories for them, both happy now that they lived in a different world. In reality Canberra was like a foreign land.

Mark happily agreed and the excited trio lined up for one of the Spirit of Tasmania ferries two days later. Now rugged up for the colder weather and with the security check over, they parked the Winnebago amongst the other high campers and trucks. Making their way to the four bunk cabin they deposited their overnight bags and made their way to the cafeteria for the evening meal, like excited children on their first outing. It was a new experience for Sophie and Pauline but Mark had done the trip a few times before and guided his friends.

Enjoying the meal amid a throng of fellow travellers, they retired to the bar for a few drinks, which of course turned into a happy drinking session. All three now tipsy, headed back to the cabin and upon entering tossed for the two bottom bunks. Pauline lost and was unceremoniously heaved up by Sophie and Mark, all laughing like maniacs. They had indeed loosened up and got into the spirit of things!

The steady roll of the vessel and their incessant chatter rendered them unable to sleep for some time. Twice because of the drinking Pauline had to be assisted down from the top bunk for a toilet break. In the end she slid in next to Mark and eventually all dozed off.

The trio was rudely awakened the following morning by the announcement they would be docking shortly and breakfast was being served. They voted instead to linger in bed and go straight to the vehicle as the previous night's revelry had taken its toll on all three.

Disembarking early at Devonport, the frost was still sparkling in the early morning mist as they made their way to Smithton to a rendezvous with Mark's eldest daughter, stopping on the way to make breakfast. Unused to the cold weather they shut the door of the Winnebago and with no power they turned on the gas top to heat the interior of the home. Snacking on toast and cheese and looking at Mark and Pauline wrapped in coats, jumpers and long trousers, Sophie burst out laughing "Fuck you look funny! I am more used to seeing you guys naked or in shorts and singlets. This is bloody ridiculous!"

"Have to agree Sophie, I suppose we have all spent so many years in a hot climate we will find it hard to adjust but it is supposed to be Spring, so hopefully when the sun comes up, it will warm up" Mark replied laughing, as he too glanced at all three.

Chapter Twenty-Two

Arriving in Smithton the sun had warmed up a little but even so, when they pulled up at Mark's daughter's home, they noticed the chill as they all stepped down from the Winnebago. They had enjoyed the beautiful drive up the coast even though Mark seemed a little apprehensive. He had not seen his daughter for over a decade and was unsure of his reception.

Confiding in both, Mark said the divorce had not been a happy event and although he paid child maintenance to his ex-wife without missing a payment, she had blamed his absence for the divorce, despite her having started a new relationship only weeks after he began working in Queensland. Mark said that perhaps he would have handled things differently if he had the chance again but that no one can ever go back and replay one's past decisions, be they good or bad. He admitted to having had a few relationships himself since the divorce but never considered marrying again. He then told them his ex, having broken up with her last partner and now being single again, had made contact suggesting they meet at their daughter's place today for a barbecue.

This came as a surprise to Pauline and Sophie who thought perhaps she was interested in more than catching up with Mark, but when they mentioned this to him, he only laughed and dismissed the suggestion outright. He promised his course was set, the relationship and friendship he had formed with them was cast in stone and assured them he looked forward to returning to Broome, buying a boat and spending time fishing and exploring the Kimberley coast with them both.

Mark's daughter Sally answered the door, instantly recognising her father. They embraced and Mark introduced both women as his good friends from Broome. Pauline noticed Sally at first seemed a little stunned but recovered and invited them in for the lunch she had prepared. Sitting around the table, Pauline and Sophie soon gleaned her three children had left home as had her husband, but her mother Roma had sold her house and now lived with her. Sally informed them her mother had a doctor's appointment and would be home later in the afternoon. She suggested that Mark show his guests around the town before it became too cold and that they then all have an early barbecue.

Checking out the small town, they decided to go for a long walk on the beach, all the travelling was starting to make them lazy. Mark, ever the comedian, suggested a nude swim but both declined joking that if they did he may never perform again!

The trio walked further than anticipated and the sun was disappearing as they arrived back at the Winnebago. After a quick shower and change they returned to Sally's for the barbecue. Both Sophie and Pauline dressed in western shirts, moleskins for warmth and Rossi boots and, because the barbecue was to be outdoors they added their sleeveless RM William's jackets and topped off with their Akubras.

241

Arriving at the house they filed into the barbecue area and although Sally greeted them warmly, the air was hostile as she introduced Roma to them both.

"I didn't think Mark would be running around the country with one woman let alone two!" she smirked.

"Well Roma" Sophie replied "we are hardly running, in fact it has been a very relaxed and happy trip. We have known each other for a long time, in fact we were both fucking him when you were home here having a fling yourself."

Pauline knew the ever feisty Sophie would be unable to act with discretion if provoked. Mark stood stunned, smiling, trying to contain himself. Roma had always thought he was useless and would be unable to find another woman but here he was with two, who looked absolutely stunning even in later age. One thing he admired about them both was their ability to tell it how it was, unlike many who would have happily swapped places with them in an instant. Never having the guts to act in other than what they presumed was an acceptable fashion but detesting those who did.

Roma stood up fuming, "Well I suppose two old hookers would do anything for a free ride, latching onto stupid Mark because he has money" she spat back.

"Let me assure you Roma" Mark replied casually "both of these remarkable women are multi-millionaires, in fact it is they who are paying for this trip and the Winnebago was Pauline's. Pauline owns one of the biggest cattle stations in the north of Australia and is perhaps one of the most competent helicopter pilots in Australia. Sophie's late husband was a renowned Surgeon and Sophie ran his practice. So from a woman who has never worked in her life, 'hookers' is a bit rich!"

Roma sank back in the chair defeated. Sally knew her mother had no savings but had gathered Mark, having sold his house and with other savings, was comfortable and had guessed Roma planned to try to win him back, simply to make her own life easier. In fact she had been on senior dating sites for some years, having had many disastrous meetings with the few viable males her age, mostly dirty old men just after a quick root and free ride.

"I apologise to you both" Roma at last muttered "just a shock I suppose. What you say Sophie is true I made my choices now I must live with them. I confess my jealousy. Sally told me you were both good lookers and outgoing, I should be the last to judge."

"Look Roma we all move on. If we cannot be friends at least can we get on? You are a part of Mark's family, so accept his choices. I assure you both he is a happy little chappy and we each adore him as a good friend" Pauline implored.

"I agree" Roma replied, more sedate now "Sally tells me of her father's exploits and here I am with no money and having to live with my daughter. When I saw you two tonight looking just fantastic, I suppose snapped."

"I am so glad that is over. Sorry Dad, I only have sausages" Sally broke in lighting the barbecue.

"We live on sausages Sally, they will be fine" Pauline advised, adding "I have a few bottles of wine if anyone is interested!"

"Now you are talking Pauline" Roma responded "I for one really need a few wines to lighten up, to be frank Sally will tell you, if I get the opportunity I am known to drink too much, I find it relaxing and a bit of escapism from my boring life."

"If Mark wants, why don't you both come to Broome sometime and stay with us. We can return your hospitality, even if it didn't start off so well" Pauline laughed.

The atmosphere relaxed with the wine having been opened and passed around, as Mark started cooking.

"Pauline if you really mean that, we will start saving, Mum and I have never left Tasmania. Seems I always had a mortgage and no money, just the idea is something to dream about" Sally remarked.

"Tell you what Sally, don't worry about saving, the three of us will shout you a trip whenever you want to come" Pauline told them both, passing around glasses of wine.

"Shit Pauline after my greeting, do you really mean that?" Roma blubbered.

"Like I told you Roma, both Pauline and I are straight shooters, a bit too forward sometimes but what we say we mean" Sophie piped up scoffing into the wine.

Pauline watched both Roma and Sophie gulping, not sipping the wine. 'Should be an interesting night' Pauline mused.

Strange bedfellows make good friends sometimes! Now light hearted banter and laughter drifted into the calm night. Wrapping the sausages in bread, Pauline gathered the long walk and late meal had made them ravenous and along with the others she drank too much, but after the frosty start she felt glad things had worked out. Deep down, perhaps she understood Roma's frustrations and those of her daughter. Life she reasoned may well have turned out much differently for her had she stayed in Canberra.

The following morning the farewell was far different to the initial meeting as they shared hugs all around before leaving for the trip down the west coast of Tasmania to Hobart and a meeting with Mark's younger daughter Betty who lived in the suburb of Moonah.

The trio enjoyed a Strahan cruise before finally arriving to meet Betty, her husband Frank and their son Ronald, still in his teens. It was a far different reception here. Pauline suspected no doubt, due to information passed on by Roma and Sally.

Mark parked the Winnebago on the front lawn and insisted on taking them all out to the local hotel for dinner. This was the much happier side of Mark's family, both Betty and Frank obviously adored each other and their son was doing well at school. They both seemed sure Ronald would break the mould and become a professional. He hoped to become a doctor of medicine, they informed Sophie and questioned her about the medical clinic. She spoke of working with her late husband in his practice as a Surgeon and also of her son Ayden who was doing well at medical college and would soon become an intern at a Perth Hospital.

The evening was a great success and they also invited this family to come to Broome for a holiday. Being fair, Mark promised to pay if ever they decided to take up the offer.

The following day the trio left on the final part of their Tasmanian adventure. Travelling to Sorell via the Tasman Bridge for the trip up the east coast, Mark now settled, happy the meeting with his family had ended well. Both Pauline and Sophie knew he had had reservations but were pleased that he seemed to have returned to his old jovial self, enjoying the scenery and the fresh local produce they purchased each day.

'Perhaps', Pauline thought as they cruised along, 'it is because we have no expectations of each other or ever judge each other that we get along so well together.' Now all three had for different reasons become comfortable with their lives, past hang ups and anxieties had long since disappeared. They had even discussed further travel overseas or a boat cruise. Life had indeed planed out for the trio. Mark gave both Pauline and Sophie intimacy and male backup and they gave him friendship and above all, company. Pauline knew being on your own can be daunting and relished the mate ship they all enjoyed. Even more importantly she noticed, no one dwelt on the past, all three looked to making the future as satisfying and pleasurable as possible. In her chats with Sophie, who she worked out long ago was perhaps too truthful and to the point, they spoke of their sexual relationship with Mark. Both agreed sex was an integral part of life, that it was a healthy activity and deep down the vast majority of women missed the pleasure of sexual intimacy if for whatever reason, it was missing from their lives.

All too soon they found themselves crossing Bass Strait again on the return trip home. They planned to go via

Adelaide and up the Sturt Highway to Broome. None had visited Ayres Rock so the decision was unanimous, then onto Katherine and the station. Mark intended to shed the ageing Winnebago there and, if they wished to take further trips later, they could decide what to do then.

Three weeks later the trio pulled into Sophie's house in Broome, glad to be home but feeling a little sad that the journey had ended. Pauline knew all three would find it a little hard to settle after travelling for several weeks. Even Mark admitted that after a few days he would like to return to the station to help Sonny in the garden, it gave him a great deal of satisfaction, he confided to the girls.

On the second day they decided to go for a skinny dip on Cable Beach. Having packed some lunch the trio drove onto the beach and after parking the land cruiser went for a long swim in the rolling surf. Pauline knew Sophie enjoyed the freedom of nude bathing and later, laying in the sun drying off, she looked at Pauline and said, "You know, I was just thinking, it seems a life time ago that we both worked in Canberra Pauline, what a journey we have both been on."

"True enough Sophie" Pauline replied "we both had good marriages to wonderful men, gave birth to beautiful children, now grown up and we're still behaving disgracefully" she laughed.

"Tell you what though Pauline I would not change a day, even the Abdul affair" Sophie smiled, enjoying the warm sun.

"Same here girls, we have all been lucky really but, now to be honest I am more content with you two than I have been in my entire life" Mark broke in.

"So you should be Mark" Sophie laughed "two willing old women to have it off with, but then I suppose we have a willing old man to take care of us, so it works both ways".

"That we are all happy and still healthy is a big bonus. We have been on an incredible journey. We are all good mates and look after each other, what else can we possibly ask for?" Pauline, laying back looking at the blue sky added.

"Listen you two" Sophie sat up looking at her two mates basking in the sun "we old disgusting relics still have a few tricks up our sleeves, our journey will only end in death. Let me assure you, I know what our Pauline is like, watch out Mark!"

"Tell you what Sophie" Mark replied "wherever Pauline's journey takes her I will follow and you will too, our bond is special. It was started many years ago, one fleeting, sexually charged encounter that I never forgot.

The three old friends sat warming themselves in the sun. Pauline knew time was catching up with them all but for her to date, life had indeed been an inspiring journey.

The End